BOUNCER'S BLENHEIM

Gus Beaumont Thrillers
Book Two

Tony Rea

SAPERE
BOOKS

Also in the Gus Beaumont Series
Bouncer's Battle
Bouncer's Butcherbird

BOUNCER'S BLENHEIM

Published by Sapere Books.

24 Trafalgar Road, Ilkley, LS29 8HH

saperebooks.com

ISBN: 978-0-85495-389-9

Dedicated to those unsung heroes of World War Two aviation: the pilots of the Air Transport Auxiliary.

ACKNOWLEDGEMENTS

My heartfelt thanks go to my wife Jane for reading and critically commenting on the text. Also to Katie Drew and everyone at the Ivybridge Writing Group. Their wise observations and valuable comments have strengthened the story enormously, and any mistakes remain my own. As always, Amy Durant and the team at Sapere Books have contributed their experience and professionalism. Thank you all.

PART ONE: THE NEXT MISSION

CHAPTER 1

October 1940

Gus Beaumont awoke, hungover and bleary-eyed.

It had been a fine Friday night out. Due to lousy weather, his night fighter squadron had been stood down from their routine patrol over the Thames Estuary and so Gus, with some of the boys, had decided to go into town.

The whole week had been busy. Since the beginning of October, the Luftwaffe seemed to have changed tactics, switching to more night raids over London. The daylit skies had been relatively clear of German bombers for a few weeks now. As the autumn weather settled itself and pointed towards winter, most of the RAF privately thought that the terrible intensity of the Battle of Britain might be behind them, though some of them wondered what spring might have in store.

The Spitfire and Hurricane squadrons could take things a little easier. They were constantly on call, but they could rest, recoup, fill those gaps left by pilots killed and aeroplanes destroyed. For Gus, recently posted back to a night fighter squadron equipped with Boulton Paul Defiants, life was hectic.

Despite a thick head, he hurried to organise himself. He threw on his uniform then rushed along to the mess for breakfast.

"What will you have, Mr Beaumont, sir?"

Aircraftman Wonnacott, the mess orderly with a thick Devonshire accent, was a good cook and an even better gardener. He delighted in planting, tending, harvesting and cooking vegetables for the young officers — it was his contribution to the war effort. And it was an important contribution, considered Wonnacott. He was forever telling the officers, "That there Napoleon, he said, 'an army marches on its stomach.' Well, so does a blinking air force, I say!"

Basic supplies came from RAF catering, but Wonnacott supplemented these with local and home-grown produce. When the squadron moved from West Malling to Gravesend earlier in the year, Wonnacott brought salted runner beans, chutneys and jars of jam he'd made from wild fruits. He served crab apple jelly alongside pork, and quince jelly on a cheese board. Best of all, Wonnacott brought bottles of homemade sloe gin, which came out after dinner.

"Good morning, Wonnacott. What's today's special?" asked Gus asked with a grin.

"I've got a nice side of bacon in, Mr Beaumont, and I reckon it'll go well with a couple of duck eggs I've managed to find and some hogs pudding I've had sent up from the West Country. Toast and jam, too, of course."

"Where the hell did you get the duck eggs from?"

"From the ducks, as it happens. Best not to ask any further on that particular issue, sir. If you get my drift."

Gus asked for the cooked breakfast, knowing he might well suffer from indigestion later. He took a seat at a table where Pilot Officer Jonny Sparling was already eating.

"Mind if I join you, Jonny?"

"Not at all, as long as you don't speak too loudly. Head's bloody spinning."

"I'm not surprised, with the amount you drank last night. You were like a bloody fish."

"It's all your fault, Bouncer."

"My fault?"

"Well, we were out celebrating your promotion, Flying Officer Beaumont."

"You have a point there."

Wonnacott arrived with the food and a pot of tea for the two officers. Sparling poured. "You've got leave coming up, haven't you? Any plans?"

"Funny you should ask… Did I spill the beans last night?"

"Sort of, yes. Something about visiting a cuddly pilot in the Air Transport Auxiliary."

"Damn. Did I really say she's cuddly?"

Sparling grinned. "No. But your description of her…"

"Oh, do stop it, Jonny!" Gus groaned. "I'm never, ever going to drink again."

"Until the next time, eh?"

After breakfast, Gus and Sparling walked down to the officers' lounge, which was empty. They lowered themselves into the large, brown leather armchairs.

"Luxury," said Sparling, lighting up a cigarette and holding the box out to Gus.

"I'll say," Gus replied, waving the cigarettes away. He'd never been much of a smoker. "Better than West Malling."

The small room was dotted with low coffee tables, each with two or three chairs around them, roughly facing the exposed brick-and-tile fireplace. Above the fireplace was a photograph of Vera Lynn, the 'Forces' Sweetheart'. On the walls hung the squadron's trophy collection. There was a Nazi swastika from the tail plane of the Junkers Ju-87 Pilot Officer Thomas Jefferies had shot down; a photo of a downed Heinkel He-111 with three of the squadrons' officers, the local Home Guard and a local policeman standing around it; and in pride of place was the propeller from the Messerschmitt Bf-110 shot down by Squadron Leader Arthur 'Keats' Holbrook and his rear gunner Spud Murphy, just before their Defiant burst into flames. Holbrook had made it out with serious burns, but Spud hadn't been able to escape the burning turret.

Gus sighed and turned to look at a map on the wall. It showed 11 Group's sectors, including West Malling, where Gus had first been based with the squadron, and Gravesend, where they now were.

"So this new girl of yours, what is she like?" asked Sparling, blowing a cloud of smoke into the air.

"She's not my girl," insisted Gus.

"But you've finished with the other one? What was she called?"

"Eunice. Yes, all that's over. Again."

Gus explained to Sparling the peripherals of his on-off relationship with Eunice Hesketh. How they had first met and become lovers at Oxford, and how she'd left him — for Murray Parkinson, he'd thought. But when he'd bumped into Eunice in London the previous year, she'd maintained she hadn't had feelings for Murray at all. She'd only picked him up to scare off Gus, because — what was it Eunice had said? Things had been 'getting too serious with you...'

"Fashion model, wasn't she?"

"She modelled, yes. But Eunice is a clever woman. I think she just happened to like clothes and, before the war, she had nothing much to do."

"What's she up to now?"

"No bloody idea," lied Gus. "Look, what is this, an inquisition?"

Gus knew he had to be careful about Eunice's past, and his own. He suspected she had been involved with Sir Alexander Peacock and was probably doing some undercover work on his behalf. Gus was in exactly the same position himself and knew how important it was to keep it secret.

"No such thing! So tell me about the new girl," Sparling persisted.

"Her name's Bunty and we've only met once. Professionally, at that. But I've sent her a couple of letters since."

"And she's replied?"

"Oh yes!"

"And she's interested?"

"Interested enough to invite me to her place for a few days. That's where I'm off to on my leave."

"Yes, you told us all about it last night! Didn't say where it was, though. Where does this charming lady live?"

"Gloucester," he said.

Gus took a train into central London, then made his way across the city to Paddington. He had time to kill before the late evening train to Gloucester, so instinctively dived into a pub. He opened the door and found it full of soldiers. On closer inspection, Gus saw that they were predominantly junior officers, and they were drinking heavily.

"Watch who you're shoving, flyboy," said a young lieutenant, his words slurring slightly, as Gus made his way towards the bar. Gus ignored the officer, who he noticed from the insignia on his uniform was a second lieutenant of the East Surrey Regiment.

"I said, watch who you're shoving into!" repeated the lieutenant, more loudly.

"Sorry," murmured Gus.

"Sorry? Oh, he's sorry!" shouted the soldier. "And I'll bet you and your flyboy chums are sorry you let us all down at Dunkirk, aren't you?"

"Not a bloody aeroplane to be seen over Dunkirk," agreed another of the officers, now egging his comrade on.

"I'll bet you were tucked up safely in bed while my friends and I were over there in France fighting the bloody Nazis. I'm right, aren't I?"

Gus looked coolly at the drunken officer, then at his compatriots. He spotted a captain of the same regiment, who looked a little more sober.

"Look," said Gus to the captain, "would you kindly call these boys off? We're all on the same side, you know."

"You could at least answer Bertie's question," said the captain, with a cold glare.

What had the lieutenant said? Tucked up safely in bed? Gus rounded on the young officer.

"You're Bertie, are you?"

"Lieutenant Bertie Moore —" he hiccuped — "East Surreys. My unit was with the 44th Home Counties Infantry Division, British Expeditionary Force."

"Well, Bertie Moore, and the rest of you," Gus growled, looking around at the faces of the soldiers, "if you must know, I was in France last May as well as you bloody lot. And I didn't have the BEF around me, nor a division, nor a battalion. No, I was on my own; but I attacked an advanced unit of German armour in a Westland Lysander, and I was doing all right until I was bounced by two Messerschmitts and my rear gunner was killed. After that I flew another Lizzie to Calais to deliver spare parts to some pongos and was shot down again. By a Bf-110. Not a nice experience to be shot at by one of those big boys, I can tell you, with all those machine guns and cannons. Then, with my gunner, I pinched a French plane and tried to get back to Blighty, only to ditch in the Channel when we ran out of petrol and be picked up by the *Royal Daffodil*, crammed with battle-weary, exhausted men rescued from the beaches of Normandy. So, please, don't ask me where I was at Dunkirk."

The pub was suddenly silent, all eyes fixed on Gus. He decided to press home his advantage.

"If you want any more convincing that I am not a bloody coward, I fought in the Battle of Britain from start to finish. I flew Defiants in a night fighter squadron, then Hurricanes with a Polish fighter squadron. So, if you don't mind, I'm just going to sit over there and drink my pint!"

Gus took his beer from the bar and headed towards the one spare seat in the pub. It was over by a window, and the route took him directly through the group of East Surrey officers. As he walked towards them, they stepped aside to let Gus through.

As he passed by, Gus felt a hand slap his back. Then another, and another. Before he knew it, the entire pub was clapping. His cheeks red, Gus made his way to the seat and forced the pint of ale down, trying not to make eye contact with the East Surrey officers. Eventually, he rose from the chair, put on his forage cap and left, to more clapping and cheering.

The walk to Paddington was only a short stroll, and once at the station Gus jumped onto the train to Gloucester as it puffed and chugged away from the platform.

CHAPTER 2

"Bouncer, darling!" Bunty cried. "Over here!"

Two hours after leaving Paddington, Gus climbed down from the carriage at Gloucester Western station and there was Bunty Kermode waiting for him.

Bunty bounded along the platform towards him, waving furiously. She wrapped her arms around him, squeezing him so firmly and for so long that Gus thought he might pass out. Then, easing her grip, she raised herself on tiptoe to give him a peck on the cheek.

"How perfectly bloody lovely to see you again!"

"Great to see you, too, Bunty."

Again she went up on her toes to kiss him. This time it was a longer, firmer kiss on the lips. Then she stepped back, took a breath and looked him up and down, as if surveying a new, ungelded horse brought to the stable.

"Blimey!" she said, looking admiringly at the Flying Officer's braid on his sleeve. "Where did that come from?"

"Suppose I must have done all right with those Poles," he lied.

Gus had acted as interpreter and liaison officer to the Polish pilots based at RAF Northolt during the Battle of Britain, but that in itself didn't warrant a promotion. Rather, it was his detective work for Sir Alexander Peacock that had secured his Flying Officer status, delivering messages to Poland before the war and, later, testing out the possibility of night incursions into occupied French airspace.

"C'mon, Bouncy dear. I want to show you off to Ma!"

With that, Bunty hooked her arm into Gus's, he lifted his small kit bag from the platform, and they strutted the one and a half miles or so through the city centre to Bunty's home in Podsmead Road.

The Kermodes' house was a two-storey Edwardian building at the end of a longish front garden. Gus gazed up at the tall chimney on the right-hand side of the house and the gables across the upper windows. Bunty paused under an arched, brick porch which, like a silent sentinel, protected the half-glazed, blue front door within.

"Here we are, Bouncy! This is home. Well, it's my home for the time being. Anyway, let's go in and see if Ma has a cuppa ready for us, shall we?"

She dived a hand into her bag as she spoke. "Always have too much bloody stuff in this old thing. Must get something smaller," she muttered as she groped around. Eventually, with a broad grin of satisfaction, Bunty plucked a door key from the bottom of her handbag.

"Here it is!" she exclaimed triumphantly and proceeded to push the key at, rather than into, the lock, her hand shaking slightly. Bunty got the key into the lock on the third attempt. Gus wondered if she had been drinking.

They walked into a parquet-floored hallway, which herringboned its way towards an open door at the far end. Gus could smell polish and guessed it had only recently been waxed.

"Oh, drop your bag there." Bunty pointed to a space at the foot of an elegant staircase that climbed to the upper floor.

"Ma!" she shouted. "Ma, where are you? I've brought my future husband to see you!"

Gus swallowed.

She turned to him with a grin. "Only joking, Bouncy. That's how we are here. You'll get used to it."

Bunty charged down the hallway and into the room at the end. Seconds later she emerged, pushing before her a wheelchair in which sat a grey-haired woman with thin features.

"Meet Ma!" Bunty declared. "She can hear us, but she can't talk. Had a stroke, haven't you, Ma?"

"Good afternoon, Mrs Kermode," Gus said, uncertainly. The woman remained silent.

"You two have a jolly good chinwag whilst I make us a pot of tea," said Bunty as she swanned off back to what must be the kitchen at the far end of the entrance hall. "Wheel Ma into the front room, would you, Bouncer? There's a dear!" she shouted back to him.

Gus pushed Mrs Kermode into the front room and placed her wheelchair next to one of the large armchairs. It was upholstered in beige leather, with brown beading picking out the stark geometric lines, the curved arms a heavily grained wood. The walls, he noticed, were decorated with similar patterns, but with the inverse colour scheme; mid-brown with lighter lines superimposed. So too the occasional tables, wall lights and lampshades. Gus was mesmerised by a table lamp that stood on a sideboard cabinet. It featured a female dancer in bronze, behind which was a beautiful multicoloured stained-glass disc. The dancer was naked and took the pose of an athlete about to throw a javelin, her long hair flowing as if caught by a breeze. In each hand she held one end of a cloth which draped behind her, creating a wonderfully balanced, curved shape. With the glass disc behind, the whole piece took the shape of a heart. The figure reminded Gus of Eunice.

"Art deco," declared Bunty, seeing Gus's interest in the lamp as she entered the room and placed a tray of tea onto one of the polished occasional tables. "It was all the fashion when my parents moved in here. My late father and Ma adored it."

Bunty poured tea into two porcelain teacups, then a third measure into a tumbler with a fitted lid, a straw pushed through it.

"Want to know the plan?" asked Bunty.

"There is one?"

"Fail to plan, plan to fail," she responded, assertively.

"Yes," said Gus, "but no plan survives —"

"Survives contact with the enemy," she said, finishing the sentence. "Yes, I know. Helmuth von Moltke. But you're not the enemy, Bouncy. Water is!"

He frowned. "What?"

"We'll stay here tonight — don't worry, Ma, I've put him in the spare room, there'll be no funny business — then tomorrow we're off to Agincourt."

"Agincourt? You are joking!"

"*Agincourt* is a boat owned by my Uncle Cedric."

"Odd name for a boat."

"His friend, Mr Rolt, has a boat called *Cressy*. I've been on board. It's powered by a Ford petrol engine and has been fitted out as a live-aboard. It's lovely — and even has a bath. Uncle Cedric always wants to go one better, so he has had his boat fitted out to live on as well. He told me the name *Cressy* reminded him of the Battle of Crécy, so he named his boat after the Battle of Agincourt."

"And where exactly is *Agincourt*?" asked Gus.

"Why, it's in the Pas de Calais, Northern France, silly!"

Gus looked at her, and she noticed his frown.

"Uncle Cedric's boat is in Stourport. That's on the River Severn. We'll drive up there tomorrow, and leave the car at a pub or something. Then we'll take *Agincourt* downstream to Worcester. Uncle Cedric lives there and would like the boat delivered. You up for that, Bouncer?"

"Sounds grand," he answered. "But right now, I'd like to know how you got involved in the Air Transport Auxiliary."

"Now, that's a story. Do you want the whole thing or just the juicy bits?"

He considered the pot of tea, top up water and small plate of biscuits on the table before them. "I think we have time for the long version."

"I'd been having some problems with men. It's not that I don't appeal to men. On the contrary, I seem to attract the attention of lots of single men my age, like yourself, Bouncer. And one or two older. I've even noticed that some married men appeared interested."

Gus smiled and nodded. He wasn't surprised. That would be Bunty's larger-than-life personality. Oh, and perhaps her attractive figure, he thought.

"Hanging on to them has been the issue, Bouncer. It didn't help that a few months ago I'd discovered Benjie Keegan, my latest, in bed with my twin sister, Maureen. To make matters worse, they were in *my* bed in *my* room, here in this bloody house!"

"Oh no, how awful for you."

"I'd left Benjie alone in my room while I popped out to get a newspaper and some other bits and bobs. When I came back, I opened the bedroom door to find them together. Benjie just muttered something to Maureen like, 'Oh bugger, I thought she'd be a bit longer than that.' Then he buried his head in a

21

pillow. I slammed the door shut and bellowed something at them."

"What did you say?"

"Something like, 'What the bloody hell are you two doing?' Maureen was beastly, and shouted back, 'Well, if you really want to know…' Then I bounded down the stairs, pulled on a coat and rushed out of the house, banging the front door behind me. I simply fled out onto the street with the newspaper still in my hand. I had to get away. What on earth was I to do?"

"What did you do?"

"Not yet," said Bunty. "You see, I could understand Maureen liking Benjie — he was so dishy. But to have him there, in my own bed! It had always been about power with Maureen. We were born less than ten minutes apart in 1917, but that was enough to give us birthdays on consecutive days: Maureen on the twenty-eighth of February and me on the first of March. Maureen spent her life reminding me that she popped out first, and so she was the elder sister — the boss. As a child, she bullied me something rotten. She copied my homework and when we received identical marks, she blamed me for copying her! It was Bernice, she'd say, and the teachers would believe her. When we were finishing at Cheltenham Ladies' College, Maureen spilled the beans on my attempts at sneaking out to see a boy. At university, things seemed to settle down. Maureen read English at St Hilda's, Oxford whilst I thrived in Cambridge, studying Natural Sciences at Newnham College. We tolerated each other when we came home during the holidays and I really thought things were getting better between us. Then Maureen bedded Benjie. You asked what I did next?"

"Yes."

"I remember walking briskly in the bright, mid-September sunshine, heading for the town centre. Chamberlain had announced on the radio that Britain was at war with Germany just two weeks earlier. Gloucester was placed on a war footing. There were sandbags stacked up against public buildings, workmen and soldiers digging slit trenches and gangs of men putting in the preparations for barrage balloon stations to protect the city from German bombs. The docks and the aeroplane factory made Gloucester a military target, you see. I dived into a café and ordered myself a cup of tea. Ma used to say, whenever you're all mixed up, Bernice, and can't think straight, sit yourself down and have a nice cup of tea. So that's what I did. I still had that bloody newspaper, so I opened it and began flicking through it. I couldn't concentrate on anything, but there it was: an advertisement urging women to join the Air Transport Auxiliary. And it made me think about just what I might do in the war. A few days later, I applied to join."

"You make it sound straightforward."

"It was, pretty much. Processing my application didn't take long, and three weeks later I was on a train to London. I was interviewed by a woman called Pauline Gower. I introduced myself and she sat me down to explain all about the ATA. She said it was a civilian organisation, but we'd all be in uniform. She told me I'd be ferrying aircraft to relieve service pilots for more dangerous work — if accepted, of course. I'd be ferrying RAF and Navy warplanes between factories, maintenance units and front-line squadrons. It sounded spiffing! Absolutely wonderful, and I told Miss Gower just that. She wasn't impressed. She said if I thought it would be fun then I might be doing it for the wrong reasons. Then she looked at me sternly and told me that before the war she'd made a living giving joyrides with a flying circus. Can you imagine that, Bouncer? She said this ATA work would be nothing so colourful. 'Do you understand?' she asked me. I told her that yes, I did, and I was sorry. Then she smiled and asked me about my background. I was already qualified to fly an aeroplane, I told her, because my godmother taught me to fly. 'Who's your godmother?' she asked. I told her it was Beryl Markham, who'd flown solo…"

"I know of Beryl Markham," said Gus. "A fine pilot. She's your godmother and she really taught you to fly?"

"Yes. In a Tiger Moth. Miss Gower asked if I had my licence with me, which of course I did. So I scratched around in the mess at the bottom of my handbag to find it. Miss Gower scrutinised the pilot's licence and looked again at me, as though not fully believing my tale. But then she said, 'Well, it all seems in order,' and handed it back. She told me that if I was half as good a pilot as Beryl Markham, I'd do nicely. Then she asked if I could start in January, and I said yes."

"And that was that? What a story!"

"No, that wasn't that, Bouncer. Later that day, back in Gloucester and still excited from my success, I decided I really must make an attempt to set things right with Maureen. There was no point us continuing to be beastly to each other. No time like the present, I thought as I reached the house. I shouted up the stairs for her as soon as I came in. But then Ma came out of the kitchen with a grim expression on her face. 'Bernice,' she said, 'something horrible has happened.'"

Gus glanced anxiously at Mrs Kermode, but the older lady just stared out of the window.

"What on earth was it?" asked Gus.

"There'd been an accident. Maureen was dead. I hugged Ma and she sobbed. Cried your eyes out, didn't you, Ma? You see, our father —" she pointed to a photo — "that's Pa, Lieutenant-Colonel Desmond Kermode CBE. He was killed in the last year of the Great War. Caught up in the German Spring Offensive, he was badly wounded as he led his men on the Aisne front and died three days later.

"Anyway, Maureen and I had never known him. All we had were the photographs. And now Maureen had been knocked off her bicycle by a lorry on a country road between Gloucester and Cheltenham. The lorry stopped and so did a passing motorist, but there was nothing they could do. When a doctor eventually arrived, he pronounced Maureen dead at the roadside.

"The funeral was a quiet affair. Close family, a few of Maureen's friends from Oxford. Benjie wasn't there, either to support me and Ma or to mourn Maureen. The vicar, who didn't know Maureen — she wasn't a churchgoer — made some appropriate comments and we tried our best to sing, but it was a funeral, after all. Then Maureen's coffin was laid to rest in the churchyard. A few weeks later Ma had a stroke, and that's where we are now."

"Oh no. I'm so sorry, Bunty."

CHAPTER 3

Agincourt sat alongside a cobbled wharf in one of Stourport's enormous canal basins. Rising from the quayside was a giant, redbrick warehouse with a clock tower climbing from its centre.

"What a place," said Gus. "I had no idea anywhere like this existed."

"That's because you don't know your canals," grinned Bunty. "There's a similar place near Derby. Shardlow. Where the Trent and Mersey Canal meets the River Trent. Inland ports, they are, I suppose."

"Now I come to think of it," he said, "there are some buildings beside a canal in London. Behind King's Cross..."

"That's right, on the Regent's Canal. Stourport is on the Staffs and Worcester Canal — built to link the upper reaches of the Severn with Wolverhampton, the Black Country and the Potteries."

"You seem to know a lot about it."

"I love the canals. And the river. Come on, I'll show you around the boat."

Agincourt was painted in bright primary colours, which Bunty insisted was traditional, but Gus wondered why a working boat such as this one would be finished off so gaily. They stepped onto the open deck at the stern of *Agincourt* and Bunty opened a small door. This lead down a set of steps into a tiny cabin with a small bed and a solid fuel stove.

"Boatman's cabin. Uncle Cedric likes it — we won't use it, though. Come on."

She led him through the engine room and the smell of oil hit him. The room contained an upright, single-cylinder engine painted dark green, which Gus didn't recognise.

Bunty saw the quizzical look on his face. "It's a Bolinder. Swedish design. Uncle Cedric swears by them, thinks they're frightfully good. Much better than Mr Rolt's Ford petrol engine. Uncle Cedric says so, anyhow. Best thing about the Bolinder is it will work with just about any fuel you can think of. Diesel, paraffin, cooking oil, even dirty old engine oil. I wonder if it would go on gin," she laughed, "but we're not going to try it. Too bloody expensive these days."

"It's the war," Gus reminded her.

Bunty went through to a small galley that opened onto a large room with a bed taking up one third of it, and a couple of chairs and a small table in the remaining portion.

"We'll both sleep in this one, if that's all right with you?"

"Y-yes," stuttered Gus, "I expect I can manage that."

"Bloody hope so," she replied, "that small one at the stern has a mattress as hard as iron." She pointed to a door at the front. "The cratch has been boarded in. Toilet's there, and a makeshift shower. If it was my boat, I'd have a proper bath fitted, like Mr Rolt has on *Cressy*. How are your knots, Bouncy boy?"

"Knots?"

"Knots. As in rope."

"Not too good, I'm afraid."

"Bugger, perhaps I ought to have pulled a sailor rather than a useless flyboy," she smiled. "Only joking. Well, if you can't tie knots, tie lots, so they say. But I'll teach you. Come outside."

Bunty grabbed a length of rope and bounded to the stern, then onto the quay. Gus followed obediently. "We only use three knots, for mooring up, and one of them isn't really a knot. Right —" she pointed to a T-bar-shaped cleat on *Agincourt* — "this is how we cleat off: go around the upright once, then a figure of eight like this, then around again. That would hold the bloody *Titanic*. Now you try it, Bouncer."

Gus undid the ropework and re-cleated it the way Bunty had showed him.

"Good. Now to tie her up, if there's a ring on land we can use, we take a line fixed to the boat through the ring and cleat off back on the boat. Got it?"

"Yes, I think so."

"Sometimes there are no rings, but little bollards like that one." She pointed to a bollard set into concrete at the wharf edge. "In that case we take a rope from the boat to the bollard, go around it twice, then tie off with two half-hitches. The two turns take the strain, the half-hitches are just to keep the turns in place. Try that."

Gus did as he was bid.

"Good show! Frightfully good — you're a bloody natural, Bouncy. The other knot is the bowline. It's a bit trickier. We'll tackle it later, I think," said Bunty. "Let's have a nice of cup of tea, shall we?"

Over tea, Bunty continued her tale of joining the ATA. "A couple of months after Maureen's death, I found myself amongst the first cohort of women to join. It was New Year's Day this year. In February we moved to the ATA's new headquarters at White Waltham Airfield, near Maidenhead. All eight of us wore uniforms; they were much like those of the WAAF, but without rank insignia. Pauline Gower addressed us. She told us that, as we were all pilots, it would make the training easier to organise. We'd progress from light, single-engined aircraft to more powerful and complicated ones in stages. Once we qualified on one class of aircraft, we'd immediately gain experience on that class by doing ferrying work. After a time we were to return to training to qualify on the next class of aircraft. So we'd progress based on our own capabilities and not according to some rigid timetable. The male pilots followed the exact same approach.

"It's a good system. It meant that as many pilots as possible advanced, but any who didn't were still gainfully employed doing essential work. Pauline asked if there were any questions. I put up my hand. I wanted to know where we'd actually be flying. She said that once cleared to fly, we'd be delivering aircraft to the front line. We could be asked to ferry any plane in a particular class, even if we'd never seen the specific aircraft before. To do this we were given a full set of Ferry Pilots Notes, a two-ring book of small cards with the critical statistics and notations necessary to ferry each aircraft. A pilot cleared on more than one class could be asked to fly any aircraft in a category. So, I'm cleared to fly twin-engined bombers, but I might be allotted a single-engined trainer. The purpose is simple: to get the aeroplanes to where they are needed as quickly and as efficiently as possible."

"I bet you've flown a larger range of aircraft than I have," said Gus.

"Probably. Go on, Bouncy boy, list yours."

"An Avro 504, Tiger Moth, Percival, Lysander, Defiant and Hurricane."

"Not bad, but I can beat that little lot."

"What's the largest aircraft you've actually flown, Bunty?"

"Wellingtons. Buggers to handle, I find. Anyway, back to White Waltham, hey? Where was I? Yes, well another hand went up. It was Dorothy Young, from Yorkshire. She asked how we would get back after delivering the plane. Pauline said it depended. If we had a fleet to deliver, we would send an

Avro Anson to bring the pilots home. If it was just the one pilot flying to a base in the UK, they'd most probably come back by train. The she mentioned overseas delivery. Well, that set off a buzz in the room. Overseas! We couldn't wait.

"I soon gained my Class Two. That's advanced single-engined aircraft. My first flights were delivering twin-seater North American Harvard training aircraft to flight training bases. Do you know the type?"

Gus nodded. "Yes, powered by a large radial engine, aren't they?"

"That's right. Capable of a hundred and eighty knots, it was by far the largest, most powerful and fastest aircraft I'd ever flown in, let alone piloted. It also had a fully retractable undercarriage, just one more thing to think about before making a landing. Soon afterwards, I took my first flight in a Hawker Hurricane and it must have been after that I flew a Hurry over to Northolt and met you, dear." Bunty paused to drink her tea.

"Meanwhile, we were all continuing our training. I soon progressed to twin-engined aircraft and got my Class Three — a light twin-engined aircraft licence. Then Class Four, advanced twin-engined aircraft. So, compared with your poxy list of six single-engined aeroplanes, Bouncer, I've flown Moths, Harvards, and Hurricane and Spitfire single-engined aircraft, as well as Hampden, Whitley and Wellington bombers, and the Avro Anson air-ferries to boot. Not a bad tally, hey?"

They finished their tea and went back to the engine room. Bunty took something from the shelf.

"Right, let's get busy. You unload the car and I'll set to with this brass baby!" She waved a blowtorch in Gus's face.

"What the hell is that for?"

"To pre-heat the engine, of course. It's a hot-bulb."

Bunty took a small stool placed there for just this moment and sat on it. She filled the blowtorch with petrol and pump-primed it. Then she took a safety match, struck it and lit the torch. Once she'd got a steady flame going, she pointed the flame onto the engine bulb to heat it up.

Gus, meanwhile, dropped supplies through a hatch in *Agincourt*'s roof, which opened above the large bed. There were two bags containing clothes and a box of food supplies. As he finished, he heard Bunty shout to him from the engine room. "Bouncy, c'mon down and give me a hand will you, darling?"

He went to the stern and climbed down the steps, into the boatman's cabin and through to the engine room. The blowtorch had been placed on a stool aimed at the bottom of the single-cylinder engine. Bunty was busily oiling various parts of the Bolinder.

"I think it's hot enough to start up, now," said Bunty, sweating slightly from the heat of the blowtorch. She pointed to a handle close to a fly-wheel. "It needs a kickstart — bit like a motorbike. Put your foot here, would you, lovely?"

Bunty manoeuvred the fly-wheel slightly to make sure the piston was in the correct position to start the engine. "Give it a smart kick now, Bouncer!"

He kicked down with his left foot. Nothing. She manoeuvred the fly-wheel again. "Try now! Good and hard."

He kicked again and this time the Bolinder caught, a slow, steady *thump, thump, thump* emanating from the exhaust. The beating of the large engine caused *Agincourt* to vibrate.

Once she was sure the engine was running, Bunty ordered Gus back onto the wharf, with instructions to untie at the stern and push *Agincourt*'s heavy wooden tiller towards the quay.

"Shout down to me once you've done that, but you stay on the quayside, will you?"

"Roger," said Gus.

"You're not in a bloody Hurricane now, darling," she smiled.

He untied and pushed the tiller towards the quay. "All right, Bunty," he called.

Bunty engaged the clutch with engine running astern, which brought *Agincourt*'s stern away from the quay and into the basin. She dashed up to the deck and heaved on the tiller to centralise it. "Cast off the bow and clamber on, Bouncer!" she shouted.

As he did so, Bunty charged back down to the engine room, slowed the engine and engaged it into forward gear. She bounded back onto deck, checked Gus was on board, and pushed the tiller to bring *Agincourt*'s bows out from the quay. As Gus came out onto the small, rear deck, Bunty had *Agincourt* straightened up and was heading for the lock which would take them down onto the River Severn.

"It's a lot of work," said Gus.

"Not once we're going along. All the engine controls are on the Bolinder itself, so someone has to run down there to sort out any change of speed. Stopping her is beastly, especially single-handed. Not so bad with two of us. If we need to stop quickly — well, we can't stop *quickly*, but if we do need to stop, I'll dash down and put her in reverse, while you stay here and hold the tiller steady."

They approached the lock at a slow speed. The lock was full of water and two workers had opened the gates ready for them. As Bunty steered the barge towards the lock, two children suddenly charged out of the lock-keepers house. They appeared to be playing a game of chase, when the leading child, a girl of about eight or nine, screamed as she slipped and slid into the lock.

A young woman came rushing out of the house. "Help!" she cried. "My daughter, she can't swim."

Gus lost no time. He ran through to the front of the boat, removing his jacket and discarding it as he did so. From *Agincourt's* high prow, Gus saw that the child was struggling in the water.

"Stop, Bunty!" he yelled, but she was already in the engine room, putting the Bolinder into reverse.

Gus jumped into the dirty mire, the cold water quickly soaking his clothes and making them heavy, pulling him down and preventing him from swimming properly. Where was the girl? There! He struck out towards the youngster, who was about to go under the surface. He grabbed her collar and pulled her back above the surface. Then, turning onto his back and kicking his legs, he swam towards the quay. One of the lock workers threw a rope, which Gus clung to with his free hand and between them they dragged the girl coughing and spluttering to the lock's side.

Once they were both safely out of the water, the woman berated the child, then wept with relief. "You're soaked," she said to Gus.

"Don't worry!" shouted Bunty, who had moved *Agincourt* closer to the lock. "I'll soon have him dried out."

"Tie up and come inside," said the woman. "We've a roaring fire going, and you'll dry out sooner here."

The child was safe and the woman calm. They sat around a fire in a small, cosy room.

"Thank you so much, Mr...?"

"Beaumont. Gus Beaumont. And this is Miss Bernice Kermode."

"Call me Bunty. What's your name?"

"Doris. Doris Wetherby. I'll make us all a nice mug of char."

"That was very brave of you, Gus," said Bunty, as Doris disappeared into the kitchen. "I'm proud of you."

"Oh, well. It was instinctive. Just wish I'd paused to take off my shoes," he said, looking at the sodden leather shoes by the fireplace. "Bloody ruined, I fear!"

"You were so bold! You seemed to know exactly what to do once you got a hold on the child. Such good swimming, too! Have you done anything like that before?"

"Just once."

Doris came in with the tea and a bottle of Scotch. "Dan, my husband, won't mind," she said, "not after what you've done." She added a generous measure of whisky to Gus's mug of tea, then turned to Bunty. "You too?"

"Yes, please," replied Bunty. "What's good for the goose and all that."

Doris poured some Scotch into Bunty's mug and a dash into her own.

"C'mon, Bouncer, tell us the story," Bunty insisted, keen to hear Gus's tale of bravery. "Who was it you saved?"

"My rear gunner. Chap called Morton. Wonder where he is now?"

"Your Defiant went down?"

"It's a long story. Do you really want to hear it?"

"Yes," said Bunty.

"Me too," added Doris.

"It was May this year."

"Dunkirk?"

"Yes. During the evacuation. I was flying Lysanders, not Defiants. Morton and I were sent to Calais with some supplies for an artillery unit defending the town. The Squadron Leader, chap called Grindlethorpe, rather had it in for me. He wanted me out of his squadron, and me getting downed by a Messerschmitt was one way of him achieving it. Well, we landed all right. Handed over the gear and got airborne again. Then I was caught by a Bf-110 that came out of the sun in a textbook attack. The RAF manual cites the Bf-110's maximum speed as over two hundred and fifty knots, but I knew it wouldn't need to go that fast to get the Lizzie in range. There was no way I could outpace the bugger."

"Crikey, Bouncer, it sounds beastly! What did you do?"

"I just acted on instinct. Like today in the canal. I rolled the plane to starboard to take it towards rather than away from the 110 and pointed her downwards. I saw the fire flashes from the nose of the Messerschmitt, felt the impact of bullets tearing into the Lysander. Then I spotted some waterlogged ground in front of me, so I levelled the Lizzie and slowed her as much as I could; next thing, I felt the impact of a crash landing. The ground was soft, and the wheels of the fixed undercarriage dug in, upending the plane."

"That was bloody clever," said Bunty.

"More luck than brains. That German pilot was too bloody confident. I must have seemed like a soft target, an easy kill. He opened fire too soon. Judging from the damage to the Lysander's rear end, the 110 must have been more than five hundred yards away when it opened fire. Luckily none of the hits were into the petrol tank."

"But what about the life-saving in the water, Bouncer?"

"That was the following day. I checked Morton was all right following our emergency landing. He was, so I got him out of the Lysander and we headed to Dunkirk on foot. The fields were flooded, but once we found a road, the going wasn't too bad. After half an hour, we came to a road sign. Using the evening sun to orient myself, I reasoned that Oye-Plage was to the west of us and Gravelines to the north. I located their position on the map and worked out that we had about fourteen miles to walk. At dusk, we approached a farm near Loon-Plage. I banged on the door. It was answered by an old man, face bronzed and wrinkled by the sun and hands as big as snow shovels. The farmer pointed us to a barn.

"The next morning I spotted a French monoplane, a Morane-Saulnier two-seat trainer, lying unused, so I decided Morton and I would fly home! As we took off we saw some figures emerge from a ruined building and run at us, shouting in French. Anyway, we got halfway across the Channel when suddenly I felt the engine misfire. Then it began stuttering and cut out altogether. We'd run out of fuel. The French aeroplane was easy to handle in a glide, but there was no way it would make it to the English coast, so I drifted the Morane-Saulnier across the bows of the boats heading to England, hoping we'd been spotted by at least one of them. The plane lost height and approached the sea; I tried to lift its nose with the intention of making a level bellyflop of a landing, but that didn't work. The port side of the fixed undercarriage hit the water first, spinning us over to the left and ditching both me and Morton into the sea."

"Good God!" cried Bunty. "What a spiffing tale. Do carry on!"

"I came up choking and spluttering, coughing out some of the water I'd swallowed. It tasted of petrol. I saw Morton go under. As he resurfaced, the shock of landing in the cold water combined with the fear of drowning seemed to overcome him.

He was shaking, struggling for breath and screaming that he couldn't swim. He began thrashing around wildly.

"Swimming wasn't easy because my uniform was soaked, like today. I got to Morton, but it was bloody impossible to grab hold of him. His incessant thrashing around in the water prevented me. So, on the third attempt, I whacked him in the face and grabbed hold of his collar, then desperately hung on to him, struggling to keep us both above water. Then I spotted a lifebuoy in front of me. One of the boats had altered course when it saw the aeroplane crash into the sea. Now it came alongside. The sailors took charge of Morton, moving him inside the vessel. They gave me a blanket and a mug of scalding hot tea. That was that.

"I left a friend there too, an old college pal, Duncan Farquhar. He was with the army and had to stay in Calais."

"I wonder what became of him?" said Doris.

"Probably dead," said Gus, despondently. "Or wounded, perhaps. If so, he'll be a prisoner of war."

CHAPTER 4

Following those few days on the boat with Bunty, Gus savoured the relaxed train journey from Gloucester back to London. He gazed at the green fields and meadows, bronzed woodland and sleepy hamlets as they came quickly into view through the window, then hurriedly disappeared. He still had a couple of days of leave to fill. Impatience had made him fit in an appointment with Wing Commander Sir Alexander Peacock.

Gus mopped the beads of sweat from his brow in the airless tube train that sped him from Paddington to Piccadilly. *A quarter past twelve*, he thought as he pulled his sleeve back over the wristwatch. His meeting with the wing commander was scheduled for one o'clock and there was no point arriving at the RAF Club early. *I'll kill half an hour in a pub*, he thought.

"A pint of best bitter, please," he said to the barmaid, and sat quietly by a window, watching the comings and goings of folk. There was a steady flow in and out of the pub, a mix of off-duty servicemen and office workers. There were women and children out on the streets. People seemed more relaxed, confident, perhaps, that the Luftwaffe's daylight raids were a thing of the past.

Gus sipped the sharply flavoured, amber-coloured beer. *Ten to*, he thought, looking up from his watch.

Finishing his pint and smiling at the barmaid, Gus strolled out onto the busy street. The air-raid siren sounded immediately. *Bugger*, he thought. The siren filled the street with a banshee-like wailing as a crowd of people dived into the Piccadilly Circus tube station. Gus joined them, fingers pulling at his necktie then struggling to unbutton his shirt collar in the sudden heat. He wiped the sweat from his brow and looked up. Crowds were swarming down the steps onto the platforms.

"Keep calm!" he called out. "No need to rush."

He wanted to tell them that there was more chance of a crush on the steps than a German bomb landing on them. No sooner were they underground than somebody shouted that the all-clear had sounded.

Gus climbed the steps, relishing the cool fresh air, and made his way to the RAF Club at 128 Piccadilly. He looked at the sandbags stacked up against the public building, but didn't bat an eyelid. Just a year before he'd seen the same defences and thought them abhorrent. Now, they had become a normal fixture. He arrived at the club just before one fifteen, and the white-jacketed steward took him through to the now familiar reception room. Wing Commander Peacock was waiting for him.

Gus saluted. Sir Alex returned the salute and offered his hand.

"Nice to see you again, Gustaw," he said, using Gus's given name.

"Likewise. It's been a long time."

"You are a trifle late. Problems?"

"Sorry, got caught in an air raid."

"Oh, that. A Jabo."

"Jabo?" asked Gus.

"Jagdbomber; known for short as a Jabo."

"Oh, I see. Fighter-bombers."

"Quite. Some Messerschmitt 109s have been converted into fighter-bombers. More a nuisance than anything else, but bad for morale. Drink?"

"Whisky, please."

"Certainly. Soda?"

"Straight. Make it a double, will you?"

Unsurprisingly, the RAF Club was largely deserted these days. Most of its younger members were away on active service, posted all over the world, and even some of the old boys had been drafted back into desk jobs in the UK. Gus could converse in private with Sir Alex as they sat in a quiet corner with their drinks.

"Do you have news for me?" asked Gus. "News of my next posting?"

"Yes. That's why I called you."

"Where is it? The Mediterranean?"

"No. Not yet. I've something else for you, to get you through the winter."

"What does it entail?"

"Before I tell you, I need you to sign some papers for me, if that's all right?"

"What papers?"

"The Official Secrets Act."

Gus nearly choked on his drink. *Blimey*, he thought. *What am I getting myself into?*

"What I'm about to tell you, Gustaw, could be damaging if it ever got into the wrong hands. Of course, as I knew your father well, I trust you. However, it's more than my job's worth not to have you sign the Act. I do hope you understand."

"Of course," replied Gus. He gave the papers little more than a cursory glance and signed them.

"You'll need to initial each page, too. Oh, and date your signature at the end."

Gus signed then handed the papers to Peacock.

"I'll witness this. Then we'll be fine."

"Sir Alexander?"

"Yes?"

"Who will I be working for?"

"For me."

"I know, but there must be an organisation. Something … some secret service. Is there?"

"Yes, but it's very hush-hush. Top secret, you might say."

"I see."

"It's all right, you've signed the Act now, and as you've done little jobs for me — er, us — before, I can let you in on it."

Gus recalled the undercover night flight over France that he'd undertaken on Peacock's behalf. He'd flown a Boulton Paul Defiant across the Channel, dropped a message to the French Resistance, and advised Peacock and Pilot Officer Hugh Heslop on what type of aircraft might suit such missions going forward — Westland Lysanders, of course.

"We've formed a new outfit — the Special Operations Executive. Still early days, but we've got plenty of work supporting resistance movements, gathering intelligence, anything we can do, really, to undermine the Germans and Italians. Anything to make things difficult for them."

"So what's it all about? This new job?" asked Gus, impatient now.

"I'm having you sent to a relatively new unit. 421 Flight."

"421 Flight? They've been based at Gravesend through most of October."

"That's right. The Flight is down at West Malling now, but they're moving to Biggin Hill soon. You'll be joining them there."

"Reconnaissance work?"

"Yes, but we're beefing it up a bit. You see, 421 are about to get nine brand new Spitfire Mark IIa's. The Hurricanes will go to other squadrons."

"Spits? Fantastic! Will I need to do a full conversion course?"

"Do you think you need to?"

After joining the RAAF as an experienced pilot and getting through initial training without a hitch, Gus had been posted to a Lysander squadron on reconnaissance and army support. Later he'd converted to fighter duties, flying first Defiants, then Hawker Hurricanes and then Defiants again. The Hurries and Daffys were both fitted with the same Rolls Royce Merlin engines as the Spitfires; the basics and most controls were very similar.

"Shouldn't think so," he said. "Give me a day or so to get used to the Spits and I should be fine."

"That's what I hoped you'd say, Gustaw."

"But why the Secrets Act?" asked Gus.

"Ah, it's like this: Stuffy has two problems. The first…"

"Hold on. Who?"

"Air Chief Marshal Dowding, of course. Everyone calls him Stuffy! Anyway, he has two problems. First is the change in Luftwaffe tactics. They seem to have stopped using their bombers as a daylight striking force. Göring's aim had been to wear down the RAF fighters. Instead, we gave him a fright and destroyed an unacceptably high number of his bombers. Now he's switched mainly to night attacks, and you and your chums are doing what you can to combat that."

"Which is not much really," put in Gus. "We generally can't see a thing up there!"

"Airborne radar is on its way. Soon, I hope. But it's the daytime raids that bother Stuffy. They often consist of high-flying fighter sweeps and large numbers of Bf-109 fighter-bombers: Jabos. Sometimes with escorts. It's probably intended to keep the pressure on us, but also to try to force our fighters to engage theirs. The Jabos can always jettison their bombs and revert to their fighter role if and when we intercept them." Peacock paused to take a sip of his whisky.

"Incoming raiders might be fighter sweeps," he went on. "These pose no threat and our best tactic is simply to avoid engaging with them. However, others are the escorted Jabo raids and some are escorted bombers. These latter two require different tactics to minimise our losses whilst maximising those of the enemy. The problem is, it's impossible for fighter command to identify from radar pick-ups which are which. Following this, Gustaw?"

"Carry on."

"The Air Marshal's solution was to create 421 Flight, a special unit of experienced pilots, with the job of patrolling the Channel during daylight hours, alone or in pairs. Their job is to identify which incoming raids are bombers, Jabos or 109 sweeps. They also pick up information on German naval activity around the French and Dutch ports — but that's a bonus. By the way, that's why I had you promoted to flying officer — you couldn't possibly go to 421 as a pilot officer."

Gus nodded.

"The Air Marshal's second problem," continued Peacock, "is how to hide the fact that we are tapping into the Germans' secret information. From Ultra."

"Ultra?"

"The codename for intelligence resulting from intercepted and decoded German transmissions. The Germans encode these messages with what's called an 'Enigma' machine. Basically, our cryptographers have busted the German's codes! Not every one of them, not completely, but Ultra has given us vital information. The RAF has had advance warning of some major Luftwaffe raids, and Ultra has also provided information on German shipping in the Channel."

"My God," said Gus. "That's bloody marvellous!"

"Now, we simply can't afford to let the Germans become suspicious of how well prepared we're getting. We need a cover. The activities of 421 Flight provide the enemy with a believable source for our preparedness. Thus, we protect Ultra."

"And the 421 pilots know this? They've all signed the Official Secrets Act?"

"Don't be silly!"

"Then why me?"

"Because I've got other work for you. I want you to do the occasional drop to the French Resistance for me. Oh, and by the way, this will probably be the last time we meet here at the club."

A smiling Wing Commander Peacock took great delight in the inquisitive expression across Gus's face.

"Yes," he said, "I've been working from some temporary accommodation in central London. Office work, you know. Not meetings, as such. But we're moving at the end of the month. Number 64 Baker Street will be the headquarters of our Special Operations Executive. You might think of us as the Baker Street Irregulars." Peacock laughed.

Gus had another day of leave before reporting back to Gravesend. The thought of visiting his mother in Winchester depressed him. He was finding her frailty and memory loss increasingly difficult to deal with. In fact, the thought of returning home troubled him so much that, after the conversation with Peacock, Gus headed instead to north London to see his cousin, Staś Rosen. Staś was serving with a Polish squadron equipped with Hurricanes, but he also had experience of flying Spitfires and Gus wanted to pick his brain.

"I want to learn everything I possibly can about the Spit before I clamber into the cockpit of one," Gus told him.

"Then pour me some more of that," said Staś, pointing to the bottle of rum Gus had brought with him, "and I'll tell you everything I know."

Staś took a gulp of the fiery spirit. "Spits are not good on the ground. In the air, beautiful. Getting her up is a different matter."

He took another long sip of the rum before continuing to warn Gus of the Spit's idiosyncrasies.

"Spits are prone to overheating prior to take-off if you wait around too long; it's because the air-intake is set behind the undercarriage leg. Once on the runway, there's a lot of work to be done. You can't see a bloody thing from the cockpit, so you use the rudder pedals to swerve the Spitfire from side to side when you take off, keeping an eye on the runway strip. You need to be ready to push your right foot forward for full right rudder in order to counteract swing effect from the prop torque created by that powerful Merlin engine. Once in the air, the ailerons can be sticky. Then you have to get the undercarriage up before the airspeed gets too high. This entails locking the throttle in climb power with your left hand then transferring it to the joystick; at the same time you pump the manual undercarriage retraction handle like mad, but keep your left hand steady on the stick as the right is pumping hard. And remember, once you're in the air, the Spit needs to get to a speed of one hundred and twenty-two knots before you can start to climb."

Gus felt his fingers ache as he jotted all of this down, occasionally stopping Staś and getting him to repeat bits of information.

Saturday 9th November 1940 was the day former Prime Minister Neville Chamberlain died. It was also a big day for 421 Flight. First the flight received the nine new Spitfire IIa's Peacock had spoken about. Then, Flying Officer Gus Beaumont arrived at its base at RAF Biggin Hill. He met the officer in command of the flight, Flight Lieutenant Paddy Green, who talked him through his duties.

"Good to have you with us, Bouncer," said Paddy in his South African drawl. "Our 'spotter' duties have eased off a bit recently, but we still have daily 'milk runs' up and down the coast. We're about fifteen minutes from Cap Gris Nez, and we send out two Spits, sometimes two pairs of Spits, twice each day. Morning and night, usually the first and last sorties of the day. They split at the Cape, proceeding either northwards as far as Flushing, or south down to Le Havre. We're checking on overnight movements of enemy shipping. We'll get you up in a Spit tomorrow, so you can get to know the kite. You've read through the pilot's notes?"

"Yes, sir, I have."

"Good. Once you're ready, I'll send you out on an evening milk run as someone's wingman. Any questions?"

"No questions. Thank you."

Gus clambered onto the Spitfire's wing and into the cockpit. He began going through the mental list of procedures he'd read in the notes and gleaned from Staś. *Turn the master switch on and wait for the dials to respond. Check that the undercarriage selector lever is in the down position and switch on the undercarriage indicator light. Check that the indicator on the panel shows green. Check that the flaps switch is in the up position. Push both fuel cock levers up for on. Turn elevator trim tab control wheel forward about a quarter rotation of the wheel. Turn rudder trim tab control wheel full forward for starboard effect. Push airscrew control lever fully forward for fine pitch. Push the manual radiator shutter fully forward to open. Using the control column, do a visual check of the ailerons and rudder control surfaces.*

What was next? *Turn on radio transmitter, four buttons, one for each frequency. Then do a quick double check all round to see that all of the above actions have been carried out. Set the directional gyro to the runway directional settings. Tighten and then check the throttle adjuster, and push the throttle open half an inch. Pull the mixture control lever fully back to the rich setting.*

He looked out of the cockpit. "All clear?" he called and waited for the acknowledgement from the ground crew. Then he flicked the two magneto switches up. Contact. Again, Gus waited for the acknowledgement. Then he pressed the starter button, holding it in until the engine fired up and was running smoothly. No flames from the exhaust stubs, good.

Whilst the ground crew were undoing the starter trolley connection to the starter motor on the starboard side of the engine, Gus adjusted the throttle to allow the engine to warm up and run evenly. He kept a close watch on the temperature gauge, careful not to let the temperature exceed one hundred degrees.

Gus fixed the oxygen mask over his face and took the ground brakes off. "Chocks away!" he called and began to taxi off. From the cockpit, he saw the other two Spits of the section move out of their bays. Now travelling along the runway, he kept the Spitfire in a straight line by working the right aileron control together with the right foot rudder pedal, just as Staś had advised. He pushed the throttle forward to increase power, felt the Spitfire's tail lift off the ground and eased the control column back a touch.

Gus held the control column steady and felt the lift as the Spitfire rose from the ground. He had to be careful; it was impossible to rush the next stage. He waited, raising the

47

undercarriage, applying a little brake to stop the wheels rotating, then waiting again until the aeroplane gained enough speed before pulling back on the stick and climbing up into the clear blue sky.

Once airborne, Gus found the Spitfire relatively easy to fly and at altitude it was an absolute dream. It was beautifully balanced, the controls were light and responsive, it accelerated quickly and was wonderfully manoeuvrable. The bubble canopy and large mirrors gave Gus excellent views, so much better than the Hurricanes or Defiants he'd flown previously. After a couple of flights, Gus was totally familiar with the Spit. He would simply think about putting in a manoeuvre and find the Spitfire had already responded.

At 1600 hours Gus set off along the grass strip as Billy Drake's wingman, with orders to stick to him like glue. They climbed to a height of seventeen thousand feet as they flew across the Channel to Cap Griz Nez. Drake banked to starboard and took a southerly course. The Spitfires were then trimmed into a slight dive at maximum cruising revs, descending to around fourteen thousand feet in order to observe the ports and the shipping. The dive and engine speed gave the Spits enormous speed, making them almost impossible for Bf-109s to intercept. After zooming over Le Havre at twelve thousand feet, Billy dived more sharply a few miles from the coast, and they headed for Biggin Hill at sea level.

Gus was enjoying his posting to 421 Flight. It was exhilarating to fly fast in the newest, most powerful version of the Spitfire. The Germans knew they couldn't catch them, so rarely bothered to try.

Then came the day he had to do his first drop for Peacock. The wing commander had explained that he needed Gus to drop a 'little parcel' into a field and had given him precise coordinates. It was a sandy clearing on the edge of some woods east-southeast of Cucq. Somebody from the local resistance would be there every morning through late November and early December.

Gus had picked out Cucq and the drop zone days before, from ten thousand feet, as he reconnoitred the French coast south of Cap Gris Nez. What he now needed was an opportunity to be sent on a solo sortie.

Paddy Green had given orders for the morning's milk run. Gus and Billy were to fly out to Gris Nez together then split up.

"North or south, Bouncer? Any preference?" asked Billy.

"Toss you for it," answered Gus, taking a coin from his pocket. "On second thoughts, I'll take the south run today."

"As you like."

The two pilots made ready for their flight, Gus having secreted Peacock's little parcel in a pocket of his flying jacket. As they climbed into the aircraft, the ground crews were ready with the starters and batteries. Engines fired up, chocks were removed and, seconds apart, the two Spitfires roared along the grassy strip and soon became airborne. Up into the clear morning sky they soared, Gus leading with Billy on his wing.

As they approached the French coast and Cap Gris Nez, Billy moved up to Gus's port wing and gave him a thumbs-up signal. Gus returned the gesture and the two aeroplanes swung away from each other. Gus took up a course due south and trimmed the Spitfire into a shallow dive at maximum cruising revs. He descended to fourteen thousand feet over Boulogne-sur-Mer in order to observe the port and its shipping — all looked the same as yesterday evening as far as Gus could see. He then continued to Le Touquet — again, nothing to report.

He then reached Cucq. Gus scanned the skies for German fighters, but could see none. He needed to descend to an ultra-low height in order to make the drop, and it was then that he would be vulnerable to any Bf-109s or 110s that were higher than him. It wasn't likely — the Luftwaffe had given up trying to intercept the fast-flying Spits of 421 Flight, but you never knew. Gus banked to starboard, taking a tight descending circle over the Channel. As he approached Cucq from seaward, there was some flak, but his low height deceived the gunners. He took a course of 105 degrees and, losing height rapidly, headed towards the forest. There it was! As he slowed the Spit down, Gus spotted a bicycle propped by a gateway, its owner nowhere to be seen. As his Spitfire lost height and began to spiral down towards the field, Gus was reminded of the drop he'd made on his own account earlier in the year — a message to his friend Professor Bloch, also in the French Resistance. He'd been foolhardy, placed his rear gunner and an innocent French family in danger, but Bloch had received the message. Today, he was acting on Peacock's orders.

He opened the cockpit canopy and, as he flew just above tree-top level, dropped the parcel from the Spitfire. As he banked to starboard and gained height, clearing the trees comfortably, Gus saw a figure emerge from the trees, pick up the parcel and walk over to the bicycle.

It was a woman and, just for an instant, Gus thought that he may have recognised her. At least, she looked like Eunice Hesketh.

CHAPTER 5

Gus stared at the older man. "Bombers? You're joking, of course? You must be."

It was December and the weather was cold. They were in Peacock's new office, at 64 Baker Street where a small coal-fire was gently burning. Gus was keen to know where Peacock was posting him this time and the excitement of it had been building. Perhaps it would be the Mediterranean, after all. Or some furtive work in France. Maybe Peacock had a Lysander flight ready, just waiting for experienced night-flying pilots like Gus.

"No, Gustaw, I'm not joking. I'm sending you to a bomber squadron, based in Greece. RAF Menidi — it's near Athens."

"But bombers? Bit of a comedown for me, isn't it?"

"Not at all, young man. Don't be so arrogant."

"What are the kites?"

"Blenheims."

"I'll need to do a familiarisation course."

"It'll only take a week or so. You'll do it here, before you fly out."

"What's my job? Bombing the Italians?"

"No."

Gus took a sip of the Scotch Peacock had given him. "What then?"

"You are to infiltrate the Greek Resistance on Corfu."

Gus almost spat out his drink. "Infiltrate...?"

"We need information, Gustaw. It's like this, we — that is His Majesty's Government — are confident that resistance on Corfu will be strong. A few weeks ago a large number of high school students from all over Corfu took part in protests against the occupying Italian army. Unprecedented bravery, that!"

"Certainly is," replied Gus.

"Undoubtedly, resistance will spread. When the Italians occupied the island in 1923, the Greek garrison didn't surrender. The soldiers withdrew to the plains and mountains of Corfu's interior. Those islands lend themselves to guerrilla warfare. The same is happening now, and they're joined by hundreds of civilians. Of course, we will support them. But…"

"There's always a 'but'," offered Gus.

"But when the war is finished, we'll need to know which side the resistance are on."

Gus took another sip of his drink. "I'm not sure I'm following you," he said.

"Some of those Greeks who stay on the island to fight the Italians, even the Germans if necessary, are Royalists. In other words, after the war they'll carry on supporting King George. But we fear there are others in the wider resistance movement who would rather Greece returned to its republican ways. Another Hellenic Republic. You know the sort? Socialists, communists and the like. Reds!"

Yes, Gus knew the 'sort' of person Peacock was referring to. Spud Murphy, his former rear gunner, had been an Irish Republican who'd volunteered to fight for the Spanish Republic in the civil war. Spud had fought as a foot soldier with the Connelly Column, part of the *La Quince Brigada* — the Fifteenth International Brigade — which took such a severe battering at Jamara in 1937. Then Spud had volunteered to join the RAF to fight the Nazis, only to be burned to death in the rear turret of a Defiant.

And there was Gus's mother, Magda Beaumont, the only female, Jewish 'liberal' in the city of Winchester, who as a young woman had been a close associate of Rosa Luxemburg. Even Eunice Hesketh had socialist leanings — wealthy, almost aristocratic Eunice, who had seen the vast inequalities at play in the British system and hated it. One day earlier in the year, they had spent the day at Oliver's Battery and seen the poor folk squatting there. Were these the sort of people Peacock was referring to? But it was no use arguing.

"Well, obviously we can't be supporting bloody Bolsheviks and Reds once we know the enemy is on the road to defeat, can we? We really do need to know who's who out there and exactly what the situation is."

"And that's going to be my job, is it? Finding out if these are 'our sort' of people, good people, or another sort?"

"Yes, you could say that. And helping your country ensure it gets the outcomes it needs after this bloody war. Fancy it?"

"Assuming for a minute I do, how do I get to Corfu from, where is it? Menidi?"

"We considered parachuting an agent onto the island, but that would be too obvious. Everyone would be on the alert. We think it would be better if you ditched into the sea and were picked up."

"Blenheims have a three-man crew, don't they?"

"Correct."

"What about the other two — assuming I don't kill them in the process?"

"Oh, don't be so melodramatic, Gustaw. You won't kill anyone. But you do raise a valid point; it would probably be best to 'lose' them somehow, I suppose."

Gus considered. The air war over England was drying up; he'd be bound to be posted somewhere else eventually. Greece wasn't a bad part of the world, the Ionian Islands even better. And, there seemed to be no way of getting away from Peacock.

"I'll give it my best shot," he said. "Count me in."

"Good man, Gustaw. I'll get the papers sorted as soon as possible. I think a few days with our Number Two Operational Training Unit at RAF Catfoss in Yorkshire will suffice. Now, will you stay for lunch?"

"Sorry, Sir Alexander, I can't. I have a date already."

"Top form. Nice, is she?"

"Very nice, thanks." Gus stood, saluted and left the SOE offices on Baker Street. He was on his way to meet Bunty on the South Bank.

Bunty had taken the train to London and they had agreed to meet by the Albert Memorial in Hyde Park. Soon enough Gus spotted her approaching the Victorian edifice. When she saw him, she bounded across the road, dodging a couple of Hackney cabs and private cars. "Gus, Gus!" she shouted. "Bouncy boy, here I am!" Once she reached him, she flung her arms around him, hugging him tightly. "C'mon, let's get lunch!"

They walked, arm in arm, to a small, rather basic restaurant behind the Royal Geographical Society on Kensington Gore.

"What will you have?" asked Gus, once they'd had time to read the menu.

"Not a great deal of choice, really, is there?"

"It's the war," he said, with a wry smile.

"I'll have the soup followed by steamed pudding and mash," she said, as a waitress strolled over to them.

"Soup for me too, then the liver and onions please," added Gus. As the waitress left, he focused his attention on Bunty. "I have news," he announced. "I've been posted to Catfoss near Hornsea, then Greece. On Blenheim bombers."

"Bombers? Has your eyesight deteriorated or something?"

"There's nothing wrong with my eyesight," he retorted, feigning anger at the very suggestion.

"Then why take you off fast fighters?"

"No bloody idea," he lied. "You know what the RAF is like. Law unto itself! Have you flown them?"

"Yes. Plenty of times, actually."

The waitress arrived with their soup. Gus waited for her to leave before asking, "What are they like?"

"Oh, they're a pleasant enough aircraft to fly, if a bit cramped. Blenheims have a very small fuselage cross-section. The pilot's quarters on the port side of the nose are so poky that the control yoke obscures the bloody flight instruments, and the engine instruments block your forward view on landing. Most secondary instruments are arranged along the port side of the cockpit, but some are on a panel behind the pilot. Like the propeller pitch control. It's placed behind the pilot's seat. You can't see it. You can only operate it by feel, but it's on a panel next to a couple of similar knobs that operate the fuel cut-off."

"Blimey! I mustn't get that wrong then!"

"Nothing happens very fast in a Blenheim, of course. Underpowered! And the latest ones have become heavier as extra equipment's been installed, though I'm sure it's needed. Self-sealing liners have been fitted to the fuel tanks, but they're not fully protected against 20mm cannon fire. I can't see that they're very accurate as bombers, though."

"Why not?"

"Well, the bomb bay doors are kept closed with bungee cords that open under the weight of the released bombs. How do you predict how long it would take for the bombs to force the doors open?"

"Now, that's not the pilot's problem, Bunty. You know very well I'll have a navigator-bombardier on board with me."

"Well, let's just hope he's good. How's the soup?"

"Average. Not as good as the mess, if I'm honest."

"Piss poor, I'd say the bloody soup is. Hope the steak and kidney pud's better. Anyway, you'd do well to remember this, Bouncer: the Blenheim's single-engine stall speed is well above its final approach speed. If one of the engines packs up on your final approach, you're done for! Bang! Will you miss me?"

"Of course, I'll miss you, Bunty darling," said Gus with feeling. "Will you miss me?"

"Prefer not to think of it, if I'm honest," she said. "Ah, here comes the serving wench with our mains. C'mon, let's not be morbid. Tuck in!"

CHAPTER 6

The air-raid sirens wailed. Immediately, Gus recognised the droning sound of engines in the dark sky. German bombers were approaching. Soon their bombs would descend relentlessly upon the city, transforming it into an inferno of chaos. Like so many others, Gus rushed to seek refuge in one of the makeshift shelters scattered throughout London's underground stations.

In the cold, damp underground shelter, Gus felt the vibrations of each explosion above ground. Sweat appeared on his brow and fear gripped his heart as the thunderous sounds of destruction echoed through the tunnels. This was different to anything he'd experienced so far in the war.

Yes, he'd been shot at by Messerschmitt 109s and 110s, ditched in the Channel off Calais during the evacuation, almost pranged a Daffy at night when he'd forgotten to lower the undercarriage. But in each of those situations, he'd been at the controls. He'd been in charge. This was different. Now, he was as vulnerable as the family that sat huddled to his left.

As the relentless bombing persisted, Gus couldn't help but think of his family home in leafy Winchester. Memories of the familiar streets and the cosy warmth of the comfortable Beaumont house seemed like distant echoes, drowned out by the cacophony of destruction. Reassuringly, he was certain his mother was safe there.

He looked around him. Amid the gloom, people smiled. Beside him, to his right, was a young woman, who looked to be about his age.

Gus caught her eye and she smiled. "Quiet night tonight, isn't it, darling?" she said with a strong London accent.

Gus smiled back at her. "Name's Gus. Just seeking a bolthole from this … this bloody chaos."

"Aren't we all? Get underground to get away from it, that's what they say. But the city's never seen anything like this. I'm Frances, by the way."

"Hello, Frances, pleased to meet you. It's strange, isn't it? I'd never have expected to be chatting with a stranger in the middle of this bloody madness."

"Fate has a funny way of bringing people together, even in the darkest hours," said Frances. "Let's hope these tunnels keep us safe."

"They will. Stay close, Frances. We'll weather this storm together."

Weather this storm together? What was he saying? He'd never met this woman before. But it didn't seem to matter. Theirs was a fleeting connection amidst the turmoil, some kind of bond forged in the heat of wartime uncertainty. And something else; a sense of communal strength seemed to emerge in that underground shelter. Strangers clung to one another, both literally and metaphorically, offering solace in the face of uncertainty.

"Would you like a drink, Frances?"

"Are you inviting me out?"

"Not quite. But I've got a hip flask here." He brought out a pewter flask from his coat pocket, engraved with the Polish eagle. It had been a leaving gift from his previous squadron at Northolt.

"What's in it?"

"A drop of whisky mixed with ginger wine."

"Yes, I'll try it. Why not?"

He passed the hip flask to Frances. "Careful, it's a bit strong."

When she had taken a drink, Frances told Gus that she lived with her parents in Edmonton and worked at the Royal Ordnance Factory in Enfield.

"And what do you actually do there?" Gus asked.

"What do I *actually* do there?" she laughed. "Sorry, it's just that I don't know anyone who says *actually*. Mostly I fit the bolts to rifles. Sometimes we also do bits and bobs on Bren and Sten guns."

"Sounds interesting."

"No, it isn't. It's bloody hard and monotonous work."

"Important work, though."

"Yes, I'll give you that. And it pays well. My wages are a real boon to my mam, what with all this rationing. What do you do?"

"I'm a pilot."

"I can't believe I'm out for a drink with a pilot." Frances glanced around the shelter. "Well, in for a drink, I suppose."

"Whyever not?"

"You know… You're a pilot what says 'actually' and I'm a factory girl from north London."

"Look, don't get the wrong idea. I've actually…"

"Actually! There you go again. What you're saying is, actually, you've already got a sweetheart. That right?"

"Sort of," replied Gus, an image of Bunty's beaming smile in his mind's eye. Then he thought of Eunice. He hoped they were both safe.

"It's all right. I'm not on the lookout for a boyfriend or anything."

"Because a good-looking woman like you already has one, I expect."

"Had. He was a solider, but he's dead now."

"I'm so sorry, Frances."

"No need to be. Albert, he was called. Albert Scott, a lovely man. And the only man I ever loved. I still do. Albert was killed at Dunkirk…"

"Nasty business."

"Were you there?"

"Sort of. In the sky and, well, in the sea too, as it happens."

"Albert was only just old enough to walk into a pub and order a drink. Snatched from me, he was."

When the all-clear siren finally sounded, Gus and Frances emerged from the shelter into a changed world. The acrid smell of burning buildings permeated the air, and the distant glow of flames made an ominous backdrop. The once-familiar landscape was now covered with ruins and smouldering debris. Gus scanned the horizon. The silhouette of St Paul's Cathedral stood resilient amidst the destruction.

"Bloody hell!" said Frances.

Gus walked Frances to Liverpool Street station and made sure the trains were still running. "You never know, following a raid," he'd insisted as she'd argued that she didn't need accompanying. Frances bought a ticket and at the barrier turned to give Gus a peck on the cheek.

"Actually," she smiled, "you're a sweetie. Good luck, and you take care up there in the blue yonder. Goodbye, Mr Flyboy, and thank you for tonight. I really enjoyed it."

"Goodbye, Frances, and good luck."

PART TWO: POSTED TO THE MED

CHAPTER 7

Gus thought he was going to melt in the searing heat.

"Come on," said Flying Officer Mike 'Brock' Linton, the bomb aimer/navigator. "The sooner we take off, the sooner we can cool down."

"Careful what you wish for, Brock," said Gus.

It was fair to say the crew members were still getting used to each other; this was only their second sortie. RAF Menidi had been home to Gus for just a week, and he was still adjusting to the high temperatures. Linton and the wireless operator/rear turret gunner, Flight Sergeant Arthur 'Farty' Apps, had been with the squadron much longer. Linton was the sole survivor of a Blenheim that had come down into the sea a few weeks earlier, and Apps had been posted from a different squadron.

Gus got the 'go' sign from the squadron leader. "Here we go, boys," he announced over the RT, and he opened the throttle on the Blenheim. The twin-engined bomber rumbled down the runway, gathering speed as the large radial engines whined. Soon Gus pulled back on the stick and they were in the air, flying in a tight V formation with the other aeroplanes in the squadron. Their target was the port of Vlorë on the Albanian coast, north of Corfu.

After flying Hurricanes with the Poles and Spitfires with 421 Flight, the twin engined Blenheim was a dreary craft, but at least it held no surprises, and today's was a relatively short flight. Having navigated them to within twenty-five miles of the target, Linton took up his position behind the bomb sight.

"Ready for the run-in. Keep her level and steady, Skipper."

"You're wrong, Brock!" bellowed Sergeant Apps down the RT. "The target is five miles to starboard; our planes are dropping their bombs there and the whole area is full of smoke. Look!"

"No!" yelled Linton. "It's the others who are wrong."

Linton had a clear view of the coast and could see Vlorë coming up fast. The outskirts of the city were clearly visible in the bomb sights. Strangely, there was no attacking gunfire. The Italians seemed to be giving their Blenheim a free run.

"They don't want to expose their position, Bouncer," said Linton. "Don't want to let the cat out of the bag to the rest of the bloody squadron. They've fallen for an old trick — a decoy of smoke on the coast five miles outside Vlorë! We're the ones who've got it right."

The port of Vlorë came up, dead ahead. Not a single shot of ack-ack was fired. Undisturbed by flak, Gus was able to fly straight and level.

"Steady," said Linton, "steady ... bombs away! Let's get out of here, Bouncer."

Just before Gus opened the throttle and steered out over the open sea, Linton was able to take a photograph. Gus flew down the strait between the Island of Corfu and the Greek mainland. He scrutinised the eastern side of Corfu, with the much smaller Paxos and the tiny island of Antipaxos to its south.

Back at base, when Linton's photo was printed, it showed perfectly their bombs straddling the target area. The bombs Gus and his crew had hit Vlorë with turned out to be the only ones from the whole squadron to find their targets.

"Hits from just one light bomber," said the squadron leader. "Insufficient to damage the port of Vlorë, so we'll try again tomorrow. Mike, tell us what we need to know."

Linton related a similar experience he'd had once before. He was navigating a Wellington in a squadron ordered to attack the Ruhr area power stations and refineries. He'd worked out a course, taking into account wind speed at twenty-two thousand feet which, according to his calculations, would cause them to drift to the north. Their orders were to fly south of Le Havre to avoid German coastal flack, but Linton worked out the drift would take them over the French port, which was heavily defended with anti-aircraft guns. He'd given the pilot an alteration of course ten degrees to starboard, or to the south, to combat the northerly drift. A few minutes later, one of the air-gunners called on the intercom to say that he could see a Wellington still steering the old course.

"Basically, what he was asking," said Linton, "was if I was sure I was on the correct route. I told him the other bomber had got it wrong."

Ten minutes later, whilst still almost on the port beam, the other Wimpy flew straight and level over Le Havre and was shot down in flames. After that, there were other times when the gunners reported actions by other aircraft which did not fall in with Linton's calculations. But he'd learned a lesson that night over Le Havre.

"You navigators," he said, "if you've checked your calculations and are sure about them, stick to your guns and never follow anybody else."

The next day the squadron went out again. As Gus's Blenheim was the only one to hit the port the previous day, they were given the task of leading the rest of the squadron. As Vlorë came up, dead ahead of them, so did German flak, but Gus was able to fly straight and level.

"Steady," said Linton, "steady … bombs away!"

Gus opened the throttle and steered to port, out over the open sea. Once again, he headed towards the strait between the Island of Corfu and the mainland.

"Bandits, bandits above and behind us!" called Apps on the RT.

Gus looked around. There they were, two Fiat G-50 'Arrow' fighters of the Regia Aeronautica. As a G-50 gave chase, Gus put the Blenheim into a shallow dive to improve its speed and soon shook off the Italian, but not before it let off a burst of machine-gun fire. *Good*, thought Gus.

"Did he hit us, Farty?" he asked his gunner.

"Don't think so, Skipper," replied Apps.

"I thought I felt something jar us," said Gus.

The Italian fighters had played into his hands; he could easily claim the kite had been hit, damaging the engines or spilling fuel. As part of his secret mission for Peacock, to infiltrate the Greek Resistance, he'd selected the beach at eight hundred feet the day before; the old windmill visible from miles away made it easy to find. This was where he'd ditch the Blenheim, praying that neither Brock Linton nor Farty Apps would be injured. The sharply rising, tree-covered hills at each end militated against a landing on the beach itself. Instead, Gus decided the better option was to glide parallel to the beach, about a half mile out to sea. Losing height the whole time, he would turn to starboard at about three hundred feet and ditch the kite on the water. Gus hoped the water would slow the Blenheim down sufficiently for a fairly soft crash landing.

Eighty knots was ideal. Anything less and the Blenheim was likely to stall. But as he banked the Blenheim to the right, Gus knew instinctively that her speed was too fast. He checked the air speed indicator. *Bugger*, he thought. Over a hundred knots. He was heading straight for the windmill and those damn trees.

"Brace, brace!" he shouted desperately into the RT and continued the descent, aiming directly at the middle of the beach. As he braced himself for the impact, Gus noticed a small fishing boat bobbing parallel to the shore, its crew waving frantically at them.

Then, miraculously, the airspeed dropped to ninety knots, then eighty. *We might make it*, he thought. The aircraft slowed yet more, descending alarmingly, Gus struggling to keep the wings level. There was a deafening crash of metal on water as the Blenheim belly-flopped into the crystal-clear sea. Water turned to steam as it ran through the cowling, showering the red-hot engine cylinders. Propeller blades sheared off and flew into the air before landing on the water to float clumsily away.

Then, with a searing screech, the nose grounded itself into the snow-white pebbles of the beach, stopping the plane's forward momentum dead. The crew were jolted violently forwards.

We're down, thought Gus, right before he blacked out.

CHAPTER 8

Gus slowly recovered consciousness. He woke to a gentle rocking motion: a calm, soothing movement accompanied by a soft lapping sound.

Gus opened his eyes, only to immediately close them again as the bright sun burned into them.

"You all right, Skipper?" asked a vaguely familiar voice.

"What? Who are…?"

"It's me, Skipper — Farty! Sergeant Apps."

Flight Sergeant Apps. Yes, now he remembered.

"Where are we?" he asked. "What happened to Brock?"

"Mr Linton copped it proper, Skipper. He wasn't strapped in right and was chucked through the windscreen. Got a cut face and a badly broken leg — I could see the bone poking through his trousers."

"Damn! What about you? And where the devil are we?"

"I'm all right. We're on a boat; Mr Linton's in the cabin. Some Greek fishermen picked us up off the beach. They don't speak a word of English, though. I don't know where they're taking us."

Gus pushed himself up onto his elbows and looked around. They were in the front of a small fishing boat, nets and other fishing paraphernalia all around them. At the stern a large man with a great black beard was at the tiller, while another man was pottering about, sorting fish and nets.

"How long was I out for, Farty?" he asked.

"Four or five hours, Skipper. This here boat came up to the beach and these blokes shouted to us. I pointed to you and Mr

Linton and beckoned them to come and help me. We carried him into the cabin and then came back for you, sir."

"Have they asked any questions?"

"I don't know, Skipper. Like I said, neither of them speaks English."

Gus rose to his feet, his head spinning. Slowly, unsteadily he made his way to the cabin opening.

"Brock!" he shouted into the confined space.

"He's drunk, sir. He drank half a bottle of brandy that they gave him. At least it'll have deadened the pain."

"Brock," Gus tried again, "Brock, how are you down there?"

The young flying officer started out of a fitful sleep and blurted his reply: "I'm not too bad, Bouncer. Leg's a bit of a mess and hurts like hell. What about you and Farty?"

"I've got a few bruises and a thick head. Apps seems unhurt. Do you speak any Greek?"

"No. I remember a bit of Latin from school — used to be quite good at it, actually. That any use?"

Well, at least his broken leg hasn't affected his sense of humour! thought Gus. *Now what about these fisher types?* Gus turned to the two burly Greek fishermen. "Do you speak any English?" he asked. "English?"

They both nodded, but didn't say a word throughout the journey.

An hour later the boat entered a sheltered bay. Dusk had overtaken them and now the sunlight was beginning to fade. Soon it would be dark. Gus looked ashore. There were a few huts, workshops perhaps, and some old ruins on a hillside overlooking the water. A rickety wooden jetty thrust out into the water. Like a compass needle, it pointed directly eastward. Slowly, the small boat came up to the jetty and stopped.

68

"Mourtos," said the younger of the two Greeks, and he pointed towards the huts as he jumped off the boat, rope in hand.

As he gazed towards the small village, Gus saw a woman walking down from one of the huts towards the jetty. The Greeks gave Linton more brandy and between them, the four men managed to get him out of the cabin and onto a homemade stretcher. They carried him off the boat, over the beach and into one of the huts. Linton winced with pain at every jolt, but he never shouted out. It was the first time Gus had seen his fellow officer's leg injury. It really was a mess. Splinted with a short length of wood and some fishing ropes, blood stained his uniform trousers.

Inside, the hut was separated into two rooms and the woman had food cooking in one of them. The smell of it was enticing. The men left Linton in the second room and went back outside, where the younger one began assembling a fire. The woman walked over to the two airmen and placed plates, spoons and a flat round loaf of crusty bread on a towel next to them.

"Drink this," said the woman, and she passed over two glasses of translucent liquid, one for Gus the other for Sergeant Apps. When she poured water into the glasses, the liquid turned grey. "I'll have some supper ready for you in half an hour."

Gus took a sip of the drink. It was fiery with a flavour of aniseed.

"What is it?"

"Ouzo. You like it?"

"Yes, thanks. Your English is very good," said Gus. "Where did you learn it?"

"At college in Corfu town. I am a teacher."

"What's your name?" he asked.

"Helena," she said. "Helena Papachristodoulopoulos."

"And the two men — what are their names?" asked Gus.

"The older one is my father, Spiros Papachristodoulopoulos; and my brother, Spiros, is the other. Spiros is a common name here. Most elder sons are called Spiros. They call my father 'Big Spiros' and my brother is 'Young Spiros'. What are you called?"

"I'm Gus. Gus Beaumont. This is Farty Apps, and Brock Linton is the wounded man in the hut."

A smile crept onto the woman's face. "Why do you call him Farty? It's a little rude, no?"

"They're just nicknames. His name is Arthur," said Gus, "which in England is often shortened to Arty. We have a rhyme in English: arty-farty. Someone nicknamed him Farty. It's not rude, not really. We all have nicknames. The other one, the airman with the broken leg, we call him Brock, but it's nothing to do with his name. That streak of white at the front of his hair makes him resemble a badger. In England the word brock is a term for a badger, do you see?"

"And you have a nickname, like the others?"

"Yes. They call me Bouncer."

"Why?"

"Because, well, my landings aren't always perfect."

"You are the pilot?"

"Yes, I'm the pilot. Your brother, he called this place Mourtos — is that right?"

"Yes, this is Mourtos."

"What does it mean?" asked Gus.

"It means the place of the dead," she answered.

The woman rose, turned her back on them and returned to the cooking. *Place of the dead*, thought Gus. *Great.* He looked on as Big Spiros talked seriously with Young Spiros. They both smoked strong-smelling cigarettes, and the smoke drifted over to the airmen. Big Spiros called for Helena and said something to her.

"He asks do you want to smoke?" she told them.

"I will," said Sergeant Apps.

Young Spiros walked over and gave Apps a cigarette. He took some matches from his pocket and struck one for the airman.

Young Spiros offered a cigarette to Gus. "No thanks. Not for me."

The older man came over with a bottle of red wine and the four of them sat down on stones or logs from fallen trees, forming a loose circle and leaving space for Helena. Helena walked over with a basin of sweet-smelling food, which she set down in the middle of them. Then she carefully ladled a large portion for each of them.

"Smells good, what is it?" asked Gus.

"Goat," she replied, "marinated in white wine to make the meat tender. Then it needs to be cooked for a long, long time with tomatoes and herbs. We call it kleftiko. Try some."

Gus broke off a piece of the tender meat with his spoon and brought it to his mouth. It tasted delicious.

"It has a wonderful flavour," he said, and Apps agreed through a full mouth.

Big Spiros spoke to Helena, who translated.

"My father says you were very lucky."

"Why?"

"He says the offshore wind slowed down your aeroplane. It only picks up in the late afternoon. Had you tried that landing much earlier in the day, you would have smashed into those trees."

The men tucked into their food, breaking off wedges of bread to mop up the highly flavoured sauce and washing down the meal with tumblers of red wine. Helena, meanwhile, took some food into the hut for Linton.

"How is he?" asked Gus when she returned.

"Weak. He has lost some blood and he's in a lot of pain."

"What shall we do with him?"

Helena spoke to her father.

"He says they will fetch a doctor tomorrow, but he thinks your friend will need hospital treatment."

"Will the Italians come looking for us?"

"Maybe. They must know your aeroplane crashed; somebody will have seen it by now. My father and brother will tell the Italians they picked him out of the water but didn't see anyone else. They might think you drowned in the sea. Anyway, if they come looking for you, they won't find you."

"How can you be sure?"

"My father says you will sleep here tonight. After the doctor has visited, we'll lead you into the mountains and onto the other side of the island. You'll be safe there; the Italians will never find you even if they look. I don't think they will bother. They're not really interested in the war. Only in bars and women."

The meal eaten, Helena stood and collected the plates and spoons. "You want coffee?" she asked.

Gus studied her as she moved, taking in the sharp features of her face, her dark brown eyes and her black hair, pulled into a tight bun at the back of her head. Could she lead them into the mountains that rose steeply from the Corfu coast?

"Yes, please," he answered, "and I'll take one to Brock and tell him the plan."

"Does he want the coffee sweet?"

"Er, yes. He takes one sugar."

"I'd say medium — a sweet one may have too much sugar for him. Come to the kitchen and tell me how much."

Gus followed Helena into the hut. He watched as she took a small copper pan with a wide bottom, narrow neck and the suggestion of a spout moulded into the rim.

"What's that?"

"It's a briki — a pan for making coffee." She put finely ground coffee and water into the briki, then took a small spoonful of sugar and held it up for Gus to see. "This much?" she asked.

"If you think so."

Helena added the sugar, stirred the liquid in the briki and placed it carefully on top of an old cast-iron stove.

"One thing bothers me a little," said Gus.

"What's that?"

"There's nothing here, is there? No homes, no people, just these few huts. Yet you were here waiting for the boat. Waiting with food almost ready. Why?"

"You'll see tomorrow," she said, carefully pouring some of the hot, sweet-smelling coffee into a tiny cup. "For now, take this to your friend, then come back to the fire and drink yours."

Gus took the coffee through to the injured airman.

"How are you feeling, Brock?"

"Lousy," he replied, sweat on his brow. "Leg's bloody killing me."

"I'm sorry."

"Not your fault, Bouncer."

"No," lied Gus, knowing it was entirely his fault. His and Peacock's.

"Drink this, then get some sleep. A doctor will look you over tomorrow. We'll talk after, make a plan."

He walked back to the group, sat down and took a cup of the ink-black coffee that Helena had poured from a larger briki. The coffee was topped by a thick, frothy film. Young Spiros said something in Greek.

"Careful," Helena translated, "it's very hot. Blow the froth away from your lips."

Gus did as he was bidden and took a sip of the strong, sweet coffee.

"The froth is an important part of Greek coffee," said Helena. "It traps in the neck of the briki. That's why we add sugar to the pot; we don't want to stir the coffee once it's in the cup."

Big Spiros produced a bottle of clear liquid and poured shots of it in tiny earthenware tumblers that were little bigger than thimbles. The five of them sat around the fire, drinking. Gus and Apps chatted with Helena while the two Greek men, father and son, talked earnestly together. Then Big Spiros shouted something to his daughter, who laughed.

"What did he say?" asked Gus.

"Nothing," Helena replied, shaking her head. "It's silly. Nothing."

Big Spiros repeated whatever it was he'd said.

"He wants me to read your fortune in the coffee grounds," said Helena. "It's an old wives' tale. Silly."

"Go on," said Gus.

She took Apps's cup first, turned it upside down onto a plate, let it rest for a few seconds then turned the cup twice and lifted it away. The grounds had left three-dimensional shapes on the inside of the cup. Helena took the cup into her hands and studied it carefully in the light of the fire.

"Well?" said Apps.

"There are the mountains; the coffee grounds say you will successfully climb them tomorrow and find a place of safety. Then you'll sail away from us."

"That's all right then," said Apps, grinning. "What about the Skipper?"

Helena took Gus's coffee cup and repeated the process. As she gazed at the shapes in the coffee grounds her face suddenly became more serious, a pained expression cast over her striking features.

"Well?" asked Gus. "What does the future hold for me?"

Helena put down the cup and stood up. "The same," she said. "It's all nonsense. Look, I'm tired and need to sleep. Goodnight." And with that she walked away.

Each for their own reasons, the three British airmen slept poorly that night. Mike Linton, kept awake by the pain in his leg, pondered the prospect of an Italian prisoner of war camp. Arthur Apps had drunk far too much of the strong, sweet Greek coffee. Gus was too worried to sleep. He fretted about what the next day might bring. He agonised over carrying out Peacock's mission. He wondered why Helena had been waiting for them in a deserted village and what she had seen in the coffee grounds.

CHAPTER 9

The sun was already climbing into the eastern sky, reaching above the mountains and warming the men as they awoke. Soon the peaks of Albania and the Greek mainland were in a post-dawn shade. The view shocked Gus into silence with its beauty.

Helena had made them a breakfast of flat, round loaves of bread and ewe's cheese. There was orange juice and coffee to drink. Apps took some into the hut where Linton lay.

Big Spiros and Young Spiros made ready the boat. They tidied ropes and checked sails and fenders. They raised a sail, and, with a wave, Young Spiros let loose a mooring warp. The boat drifted slowly at first then, as the wind filled the sail, it picked up speed and set off to the south. They were going to fetch the doctor.

As the sun rose, the heat of the day intensified. Gus sweated doing little. Apps became uncomfortable, mopping his brow with his cap and scratching at an itch. Gus turned towards the hill at a sound and saw two burly young men dressed in long-sleeved shirts, leggings and calf-length leather boots. Their heads were wrapped in close-fitting, turban-like headdresses. Each carried a brightly coloured knapsack, Italian rifles slung over their shoulders. The men walked down a path and towards the huts. Helena greeted them with waves and smiles. She spoke to them in Greek and the men went into one of the huts.

"Nikos and Dimitri," she explained. "They've brought you some things. Hats to keep off the sun, water bottles and bags to carry your loads."

"Thanks," said Gus, "but we don't have that much luggage with us."

"No, but you'll help carry these." She pointed towards Nikos and Dimitri, who reappeared from the hut, each carrying one end of a large box. Placing the box on the ground, Nikos took a crowbar to lever off the lid. Inside were Lee-Enfield rifles, brand new SMLEs exactly the same as those which equipped the British army. Gus realised why the fishing boat had come to Mourtos yesterday, and why Helena had been waiting there for them. Nikos and Dimitri returned to the hut and came out with a second box. It contained ammunition.

The boat returned at about five o'clock. Alongside Big Spiros and Young Spiros was a tall, much older man dressed in a dark suit and wearing a black fedora. The three of them clambered ashore and walked over to Gus and Apps. The newcomer offered his hand and introduced himself in slow, heavily accented English.

"Young men," he said, "I am Doctor Andreas Nicolaides. On behalf of the islanders of Corfu, I thank you for supporting our country. Your sacrifice is very much appreciated. Now, where is the patient?"

Gus took the doctor into the hut and left him there with Linton. After a few minutes, during which Linton's screams could be heard, Doctor Nicolaides returned to the airmen, who were drinking coffee.

"The leg is badly broken, and it's already showing signs of infection. He certainly needs to be in a hospital. I'm sorry. It also means that your comrade will have to be handed to the Italians."

"What?"

"It is the only option. He's too badly injured to hide away with you two. The only hospital is in Corfu town. The Italians will look after him, treat his wounds. Then he'll be held as a prisoner of war."

Gus rose. "I'll tell him."

He walked over to the hut with two cups of coffee. Inside, Linton was awake, looking depressed.

"You need to go to hospital, Brock," Gus said, handing Linton a cup of coffee.

Linton sighed heavily. "I know. Does that mean handing me over to the Italians?"

"I'm afraid it does. No alternative. They'll get you sorted out."

"Yes, and I'll be a prisoner of war for the bloody duration. Not the war I thought I was going to fight. Actually, Bouncer, my war's over, isn't it?"

Gus nodded. "Sorry, old man."

"If I give you an address, can you get a message to my folks? Tell them what happened and that I'll be fine?"

"Of course I will. I'll fetch some paper."

Gus, relieved to have an excuse to leave him, went to fetch a pen and paper from the Greeks. A little later, Linton was carried out of the hut, placed on board the fishing boat and bidden farewell by Gus and Apps. Off he went into the distance, accompanied by the fishermen and Doctor Nicolaides.

The load of rifles and ammo was divided between the five of them. Helena gave them each a small package of food for the journey. As the sun began to set behind the western peaks, the small group trudged off into its fading light, towards the looming hulk of Mount Pantokrator.

Nikos led the way. Behind him, Gus walked with Helena. Apps, who did not cut the figure of a lithe mountaineer, lagged at the rear with Dimitri. By eleven o'clock the moon was high in the dark Ionian sky, and it had become clear to them all that Apps was struggling.

"We won't make it to the west coast tonight with him," said Helena.

"I'm not leaving him."

"No. We'll need to camp somewhere. I'll ask Nikos."

She picked up speed to close on Nikos whilst Gus allowed Apps and Dimitri to catch him up.

"How are you doing, Farty?"

"I'm too bloody hot, and too bloody fat! Let's face it, Skipper, I'm not cut out for this sort of thing."

At least, thought Gus, the two of them were wearing tropical flight dress, cotton twill and shorts. With the brimmed hats provided by the Greeks, they were reasonably well equipped — though their boots wouldn't last too long on the dry, stony paths they were walking along. It was Apps's physique and fitness that was letting him down.

"Don't worry, Farty, we'll take a tea break soon."

"And a smoke, Skipper?"

Gus grinned. "And a smoke."

Once the group had cleared the summit of Pantokrator, Nikos altered course and swung to the south-west. They halted on the far side and found some cover in a deserted olive grove. Four of them sat themselves down to rest, whilst Dimitri kept watch. The British flyers drank copious amounts of water, but just picked at the bread and cheese.

"Nikos says you need food; we still have far to travel," said Helena. "Try this."

She passed them two pieces of a thick brown substance. Gus spotted seeds in it.

"What is it?"

"Fig pie. Try some."

Gus took a small bite of the fig pie. It was intensely sweet, with a flavour he didn't recognise. Spicy, sightly hot. It was good.

"Tastes nice, thanks."

"I'm pleased you like it."

Gus forced down some of the bread and drank more water, making sure Apps did likewise.

"Where are we heading?"

"We are making for the hills near Ermones. We'll stay here until he's rested, then walk again until the early morning. Nikos says we'll camp on the Ropa Plain during the day and continue our trek tomorrow night."

The grass of the plain was knee-high and full of flowers. As they walked through it, Gus noticed his legs itching and cursed his RAF tropical shorts — probably ticks. As dawn broke and the sun rose behind them, Gus saw there were more mountains ahead. A small village was perched halfway up the closest of them.

"That's Vatos," said Helena. "We'll need to skirt around it, but not until tonight. We'll stop soon and spend the day on the plain."

At the far end of the plain was an olive grove where Nikos halted them once again. Apps removed his boots to reveal feet that were red, swollen and blistered. Dimitri produced a flask of ouzo, not to drink but to dab onto the ticks, so that they could easily be picked off.

They dozed during the day. An aeroplane flew over them.

"Is he looking for us?" asked Apps.

"Maybe," said Helena.

"No. It's a Macchi C-202 Folgore. One of the Italians' newer fighters," said Gus. "The pilot's not likely to be looking for anyone. They'd send up a reconnaissance plane to look for us, if they were going to."

"In any case," said Helena, "we can't be seen under this cover."

In the afternoon Nikos and Dimitri set out and returned with two rabbits and some onions. The men lit a fire and produced a cooking pot. Helena peeled onions and skinned and gutted the rabbits, jointing them and adding them to the pot. Later she produced a bubbling stew.

"Rabbit stifado," she said. "It's very good."

"Bloody hell," said Apps, "first goat and now rabbit. What would my missus have to say?" But he ate heartily and drank the red wine with gusto.

The next night they walked, or limped in Apps's case, from the Ropa Plain, taking a track that took them north of Vatos. Then the slog up Mount Georgios began. They avoided the summit by taking a small, winding track to the left of it. Eventually, Nikos began to lead them down a narrow, slippery path, which brought them to a deserted sandy beach.

"Mirtiotissa," he said, with satisfaction.

"We are here," said Helena.

"What now?" asked Gus.

"We wait. The Italians never come here. They don't often come to the west coast at all, and here, it's far too remote. Later today an andarte boat will come for the rifles and ammunition."

"Andarte?"

"The resistance," she answered, then, "Want to swim?"

Nikos and Dimitri had walked away to the northern end of the beach, probably to catch more rabbits, Gus thought. Why not go for a dip? The deep blue Ionian sea looked inviting.

"All right," he said. "Come on, Sergeant Apps, strip down to your shorts and get yourself into the water."

"Not for me, Skipper. Can't swim."

"Then at least get your feet in for a paddle. It'll do them the world of good!" Gus had removed his boots and socks and was stripping off his jacket and shirt as he spoke.

"If you say so, Skipper," said Apps, and he reluctantly sat down to take off his boots.

By the time Gus waded back out of the sea, Nikos and Dimitri had returned with fish. There were five of them, enough for one each. They gutted the fish, doused them with olive oil, then threaded them onto a stick. Dimitri rigged a spit over an open fire and turned the fish slowly until they were cooked through.

"We've run out of red wine," said Helena, "but we have retsina. The bottles have been in the sea, so they should be chilled by now."

Gus took a swig. It tasted bitter, but was refreshing nevertheless. "What is it?"

"Retsina. White wine flavoured with pine sap. Do you like it?"

"Not bad," said Gus, as Apps spat out a mouthful.

"Sour as!" he complained.

"The andarte will bring us more supplies," Helena said comfortingly.

"When will they be here?" asked Gus.

"Soon."

CHAPTER 10

"Good morning, gentlemen." The confident voice cut through the morning mist like an axe slashing through a tree trunk. A solitary figure, tough and agile, strode up to the camp. Gus noticed two pips on each epaulette of the well-worn but still smart Greek army uniform he was dressed in.

Taking a few steps forward and slinging the Italian sub-machinegun over his shoulder, the robust-looking lieutenant turned to Dimitri. "If I were a squad of Italians, you'd be dead meat by now. Sharpen up!"

"Yes, sir."

The officer then turned to Gus, raised his hand in salute, and said in heavily accented English, "Allow me to introduce myself. I am Lieutenant Nicolaides, 10th Infantry Regiment of the Greek Army, currently Commanding Officer of the Corfu Andarte. And you gentlemen are?"

Gus sprung to his feet and returned the salute. "Flying Officer Gustaw Beaumont, Royal Auxiliary Air Force, and this is Flight Sergeant Apps. Pleased to meet you, Lieutenant."

So, thought Gus, *the andarte was here*. It hadn't arrived as soon as Helena had predicted, but when it had arrived, it was overland rather than by boat and, to his surprise, it seemed to be just one man.

"Good to meet you, too. My Christian name is Yannis."

"At least it's not another blooming Spiros," muttered Apps.

"Ha!" The lieutenant smiled. "You noticed that? We have too many named Spiros on this island."

"I'm Gus, but my friends call me Bouncer." Gus shook hands with Yannis.

"You were shot down by Italian fighters?"

"Yes. Caught some fire returning from a raid. Had to ditch the kite. Bloody nuisance!"

"You were lucky. Lucky to land in one piece and lucky my friends were the first to find you. They are looking after you?"

"Yes, splendidly. My navigator has a badly broken leg, though. He's been handed over to the Italians."

"I know. My father, Doctor Nicolaides, examined him the other day."

"We really need to get back to base, if you think that's possible," said Gus.

"Where are you based?"

"RAF Menidi. It's near Athens."

"I know where it is — this is my country."

Gus looked abashed. "Sorry."

"It's a long way, but we could have managed it. Now it's impossible."

"Why?" asked Gus.

"I'm afraid I bring some bad news, Bouncer."

"What bad news?" asked Helena.

"I was in Gouvia a couple of nights ago, sitting in my father's house listening to a broadcast from Athens Radio. The city has fallen to the Germans."

"What? Are you sure?"

"Absolutely sure." Yannis spat on the ground. "The radio announcer reported that the Germans drove straight to the Acropolis and raised their damned Nazi flag over it. I couldn't believe it at first. I asked my father, how this could happen?"

"If Athens has fallen, then Greece will fall," said Helena.

"The voice on the wireless urged us to stand firm! 'Stand proud and dignified,' he told us. He insisted Greece will live again and will be great, because we fought honestly for a just cause. For freedom. 'Have courage and patience,' he said. 'Be stout-hearted and we will overcome these hardships. We have been an honest nation and have brave soldiers.' He was speaking as though we're already beaten."

"Oh my God! Then we are doomed!" said Helena.

"Damn," said Gus.

"Shit and double shit," said Farty Apps.

The angered Yannis was unmoved by their astonishment. "If I had my way, I'd have ordered the army into the mountains right then to join us. I fought the Italians on the mainland last year, and we pushed them back into Albania. The Italians don't fight well in the mountains. Look at Corfu; it's all mountains and coastline — rocky bays, caves, high peaks and mountain passes. In the last century our ancestors and the Souliotes fought Ali Pasha and the Ottomans in these mountains. We can beat the Italians here. They will never find a small group of well-armed partisans in this rocky wilderness, and we can still get you away. Get you to Crete."

"Crete?" asked Gus.

"Yes. That's where they are heading, the English."

"How can you get us away?"

"Fishing boats. One from here to Lefkas. Then to Kefalonia. Then to Zante, and then... Well, it's still a long way to Crete, but that's where the English are retreating to. We can do it!"

Having lost Mike Linton, Gus was determined to get Apps safely away. In the back of his mind were Peacock's words about the Blenheim crew; *It would probably be best to lose them, somehow.* He needed to ditch Farty, and quick. Gus himself, however, needed to stay. He had to win the trust of the andarte and get the information Peacock wanted.

Nicolaides's voice brought Gus back to the present. "But there is a favour we need to ask of you first, Bouncer."

"What favour?"

"Helena tells me you are a pilot. We need you to steal an Italian aeroplane and bomb the runway so that they can't use it against us."

All eyes were on Gus.

"Oh, take that astonished look off your face, Bouncer! We can do it," laughed Yannis. He went on to explain about the Italians' self-sufficient force of tanks and motorised infantry with aerial support. He made it clear that the andarte could match the Italians on the ground, but air reconnaissance and aerial tactical bombing would wipe out his partisans.

"I'll give it a go," said Gus. *It'll give me a chance to get closer to the andarte*, he thought, *and who knows, the hare-brained idea might even work.*

"Good," said Yannis. "I'll show you the aeroplanes tomorrow."

"But there's no place for my flight sergeant in that sort of operation. I need you to get him away." Gus turned to Apps. "You must get to Crete, find our squadron, or any RAF unit, and tell them that Flying Officer Linton is a prisoner of war and I am helping the Resistance here."

"But what about you, sir?" Apps protested.

"I'll follow just as soon as I can."

Preparations were made for Apps to depart later that day. A boat arrived for him, and Helena gave him a package of food for the journey. The men loaded the flight sergeant with bottles of retsina and ouzo.

"Make sure some of that gets to the bloody officers' mess, Farty!" shouted Gus as the ropes were slipped and the small boat floated away from the beach.

"Oh, it will, Mr Beaumont, sir. I'll give all this retsina to the officers and make sure the strong stuff finds its way to the sergeants' mess!"

With that, Flight Sergeant Apps, content to be away from the travails of the mountains, set off on a convoluted sea journey from Corfu to Crete.

A fire was set, a meal was served and Gus, Yannis and Helena sat down to eat.

"What do we have tonight?" asked Gus.

"Kleftiko again," replied Helena.

"Bandit food, we call it. It's goat," explained Yannis. "It's cooked very slowly on a low heat, with potatoes and vegetables. The slow oven makes no smoke; that way, the bandits of the past could cook and not be spotted."

"And the andarte of today," added Helena as she served up the food.

Three single-seat, Breda Ba-65 ground-attack aircraft sat on the grassy strip close to Gouvia. Gus, lying unseen in long grass, thought them ugly. About the size of a Hurricane, though nowhere near as streamlined, the huge eighteen-cylinder twin-row air-cooled radial engine dominated the aircraft's features. The cockpits were situated well forward in comparison with the wing, which he guessed gave the pilot a good downwards view much favoured in a ground attack. Gus searched his memory for information about the Italian bomber. Maximum bomb load was about one-thousand pounds, he thought, and they sported four machine guns. Importantly, the Ba-65 had a range of more than three hundred miles on a full tank of petrol.

"Will you be able to fly one?" asked Yannis.

The two of them were lying down in the scrub, gazing at the aeroplanes. Two guards were drinking coffee in a small shed at the entrance to the makeshift base.

"Yes. Most kites are pretty much the same in their basics. Starting it will be tricky. I don't suppose any of your andarte will have acted as ground crew before?"

"There is a man loyal to us who worked as an engineer at Kapodistrias airport, before the Italians occupied it. I'll fetch him when we're ready."

"That's good. How will we know the planes are fuelled and armed?"

"I'll have lookouts posted regularly. They will report to me twice a day. First, we'll detect a pattern and make a plan around it. Then we'll keep the lookouts in place to double check. Come on, we've seen enough. Let's get back."

The route back to the partisans' base took the pair through olive groves and around mountains, through ravines and eventually down the dusty path to the camp.

"Before you steal the aeroplane and bomb the Italians," said Yannis, "we are planning on attacking them on the ground. Would you like to join us?"

What was this? A test? A challenge?

"What do you have in mind?"

"In a few days we are going to ambush an Italian column. Would you care to join us?"

"Yes," said Gus, without hesitation.

"That's good. Can you handle a rifle?"

"I did some shooting when I was younger, but I'm no expert."

"The Lee-Enfield isn't hard to use. I'll show you," said Yannis, "but we can't practise with live ammo. Can't afford to waste it. You can dress like us; I have spare clothing."

"No," said Gus. "If I'm going to fight the Italians, I'll fight them in a British uniform."

"Your choice, Flying Officer Beaumont, and a good one in my opinion!"

The Corfiot andarte's superb intelligence system told Yannis and Gus that Major Sartori had split his force into two. Sartori himself had taken the main part south, leaving Lieutenant Apiro to lead a smaller force north towards Gouvia and Ypsos. The andarte hatched a plan to attack this smaller force.

The early summer sun was beginning to fall, and dusk was rapidly approaching. Gus watched from the scrub as the Italian convoy led by two Fiat 3000 tanks trundled towards him. These were followed by a couple of trucks, each containing a dozen Italian troops, plus drivers and machine-gunners. With the tank crews, Gus counted over thirty Italian soldiers. A relatively small force, but a strong one.

The last truck of the convoy had just rounded a bend when Gus noticed the leading tank slow down to a crawl. He heard an Italian officer shout, probably asking what the problem was. Gus could see clearly what was happening. There was someone in the road. It was a uniformed soldier, his left arm in a sling. The Italians shouted and gesticulated; they thought it was one of their men.

The convoy had slowed even more, and the leading tank came to a halt. As the tank stopped, the figure in the road threw a grenade at it.

It wasn't an Italian soldier standing there. It was Yannis Nicolaides. He wore a captured Italian officer's tunic, knowing the sight of a uniformed man in that dwindling light would cause confusion. His planning was perfect.

Gus watched as the grenade exploded on the side the tank, badly injuring a soldier. Then terrific gunfire erupted from each side of the road as the andarte hiding in the ditches opened fire. Soon a savage close-quarters fight broke out, the leading Italians pinned down in their tanks.

An Italian voice barked orders, but these soldiers hardly needed to be told. These were handpicked, experienced and well-trained men, and they responded quickly. Each man took up a position offering as much cover as possible, then they opened up a storm of rifle fire which surprised the andarte.

Gus and the andarte continued firing, but soon the Italians' bullets began taking their toll.

"Stavros is hit!" someone cried.

"Keep firing. How bad is he?" replied Demis, who Gus had worked out must be second in command.

"Not breathing. He's gone."

"Bastards," breathed Demis as he pushed another clip into the Lee-Enfield and carried on shooting at the Italians.

"Keep firing! Keep their heads down!"

Demis saw that the andarte to his right, led by Yannis, had launched themselves at the first truck. Italian soldiers, shot dead or caught by grenades, lay in the road. Some were wounded. Others were now being killed with rifle butts and bayonets.

"Keep firing, men," urged Demis.

For the next few minutes there was intense rifle fire along that lonely stretch of road between Corfu Town and Gouvia. Demis and Gus kept their andarte riflemen firing and Yannis had positioned his men so that the Italians were pinned down. But Apiro urged on his soldiers, who returned fire with well-practised rapidity. It was a stalemate.

"Cease fire!" Yannis shouted, and after a short time all the gunshots stopped. The air was silent, the poor light fading into thick gloom. Full darkness was not far away.

"Will you surrender?" shouted Yannis. "If you agree, we'll take your weapons, set the vehicles alight and leave you be. What do you say?"

Yannis has had enough, thought Gus.

"Yes, we do!" called back an Italian voice. "We surrender. Put down your weapons, men."

On hearing the call of surrender, the Italians dropped their rifles and raised their arms above their heads.

"Demis, take two men and get their weapons."

Two andarte emerged from cover and walked slowly towards the Italians' position. One of them stood in front of an Italian who had thrown his rifle down onto the ground in front of him.

"Hands up!" he ordered.

For a moment, nobody moved. Then the Italian quickly reached for the revolver in his belt and in a single movement shot the andarte soldier in the stomach. His comrades were transfixed, dumbstruck by what had happened. While they looked on in a state of shock, the Italian aimed his revolver at another young andarte, and opened fire. The boy fell to the ground. The Italian soldiers then retrieved their weapons and resumed their shooting.

"Bloody hell!" said Yannis. "Open fire again!" He jumped up and fired four or five shots from the Lee-Enfield. "Keep their heads down, Demis. I'm going out to get those lads."

"Not on your own, you're not," muttered Gus, jumping up. Together they sprinted out towards the two andarte who now lay on the ground in front of the Italian position. A big Italian charged at Gus and tried to club him with a rifle butt. The airman ducked down to his left, swung right and shot the man in the belly. The Italian fell to the ground as Gus ran onwards. Yannis, meanwhile, taking temporary cover behind the cab of a tank, had shot two Italians; killing one, he thought, and winging the second. Gus came upon the body of an andarte volunteer, with another crouched beside him. The wounded man was still breathing and moaning.

"Yannis, come here and lend me a hand, will you?"

As the others led by Demis gave them covering fire, Gus and Yannis brought the wounded man back to the andarte line by dragging him along the road.

"He's badly wounded, and another is dead."

"Rapid fire," shouted Yannis, "and don't stop until I tell you!"

The road erupted once more in a blaze of rifle and pistol fire.

"Those evil bastards!" said Yannis. "I've never seen that before, a deliberate false surrender."

"Well, we've seen it now," replied Gus, "and it looks like they're about to try it again, look!"

A white handkerchief could just be made out in the gloom. "We surrender!" shouted a voice.

"Piss off! Italian scum!" shouted Yannis in reply. "You've cheated once and deserve to die! Carry on firing, men! Kill the Italian bastards!"

Yannis kept the andarte firing at a range of only ten yards, sometimes less, until he was confident all the Italians were dead. Even then, it was difficult to call his enraged men off.

"Stop!" shouted Yannis as one andarte was bayoneting a body on the ground.

"Stop! The fight's over!"

A silence descended over the brutal scene. Gus swore he could smell blood and death amongst the cordite.

"Two dead and one wounded. I don't think he will make it. The lads are badly shaken up. Three of them are over there, throwing up. Just look at them," said Demis.

"Drill them, Demis."

"Drill them? Are you sure?"

"Yes, I'm bloody sure! These boys are high as kites on the taste of death! We need to calm them down. Make them form up and perform drill. Then we'll march them away like soldiers. I am a Greek soldier, and Flying Officer Beaumont here is a British airman. What we both value most is discipline. Am I right, Gus?"

"We certainly do value discipline," agreed Gus.

"In any army, and in my andarte column for certain, discipline is everything!"

Two Fiat tanks and two trucks were destroyed by fire, their burnt-out wrecks blocking the roads for days. Twenty-eight Italian soldiers, handpicked, well trained and superbly equipped, lay dead at the scene. These included the officer commanding them, Lieutenant Roberto Apiro.

Four of the Italians had somehow survived the skirmish. Demis had disarmed one of them and was walking him up the road as a prisoner. A single shot sounded. That made twenty-nine dead.

Gus and Yannis later heard that one of the wounded Italians, Sergeant Luca Conti, had managed to escape from the ambush site and had asked for help at a nearby house. Unbeknownst to him, two of the andarte were staying there. They shot him dead with his own gun and his body was dumped in Gouvia bay. Thirty dead. What happened to the other two Italians, nobody knew.

CHAPTER 11

A week later an agitated Young Spiros was brought to the camp by one of the andarte guards. "I have some bad news. Doctor Nicolaides has been arrested," he blurted.

"Calm down and tell us exactly what happened," said Yannis, as Helena began murmuring translations so that Gus could follow the conversation.

"After taking the wounded Englishman to Corfu, my father and I returned to our work. One day we were fishing in the bay. There was some commotion, so we sailed to shore to find out what it was. We spoke to his neighbours. They were woken by banging and shouting at his front door. Before he could get down to answer, Italian soldiers broke in. The neighbours heard it all. My father sent me to deliver the news to you. I knew one of your men would find me and bring me here."

"That's how they do it," said Yannis, frowning, "always like that, in the early hours. Catch people when they are half-asleep, unready. Carry on, Spiros. Tell us all the detail you know."

"An officer pushed through the throng of noisy soldiers. He shouted at your father, demanded to know if he was Doctor Andreas Nicolaides. 'What if I am?' said the doctor. 'Are you Doctor Andreas Nicolaides?' the officer insisted. He said yes, and the officer told him he was under arrest.

"Your father's friend, Alex Constantinos, saw most of it. He heard your father ask what he was supposed to have done. The officer didn't answer. He nodded to a corporal, who swiftly bound the doctor's hands behind him. He was taken away in an army lorry.

"Alex watched as the Italians drove away. Then he sent his nephew to follow at a safe distance on his bicycle. Later the boy returned and told his uncle that the doctor had been taken to the Italian headquarters in Corfu town. Alex got this news to us."

"What will they do to him?" asked Helena.

"Question him. Torture him. Maybe do nothing, just hold him."

"Can we get him out?" asked Gus.

"Impossible," answered Yannis. "The Italians are holed up in easy-to-defend buildings inside the old city. It was built with defence in mind. We can't get him out."

"So, we can't do a thing?" Helena seemed on the verge of tears.

"We could kidnap one of them? Do an exchange?" suggested Gus.

Yannis was speechless. Helena gave a nervous giggle. Yannis called Nikos and Dimitri over and barked at them in Greek. The partisans became animated, excited, all speaking at the same time.

"They think it's worth a try," said Yannis, "and if we're going to kidnap an Italian, we'll go for Colonel Zola himself."

The plan was a direct response to the Italians' actions. Gus and the andarte considered it justified.

Within the hour the partisans had come up with a plan. Zola's battalion headquarters was in a first-storey suite of rooms in an old stone building on the Liston colonnade. Every morning the colonel travelled there in a chauffeur-driven car from his residence a few kilometres away, situated on the end of a small peninsula to the south-east of the town. The route went along the Dimokratias, a little-used coast road that ran from a breakwater north of the Mon Repos and into the Old Town. For a long stretch, the road had only trees on one side and the sea on the other. After work, Zola preferred to dine alone, usually in a handy taverna in town. The chauffeur would drive him home afterwards. Both Zola and his chauffeur carried handguns.

"We'll set up a roadblock on the Dimokratias," said Yannis, going through the plan. "Some of our men will tail Zola to wherever he dines. They will wait for him to come out, and make sure it's just him and the driver in the car. Then they will signal us."

"How will we do the signalling, Yannis?" Gus asked.

"Radio from the pair tailing him to a fixed point above the Dimokratias. The man there will signal to us with flashlights. We'll need Italian uniforms and weapons. We stop the car — nothing unusual in that — and ask for papers. When Zola reaches for his ID, we open the doors, cosh them both, then jump in the car. Can you drive, Gus?"

"Yes, I can."

"Then you and I can do the job. Zola speaks good English, so you can talk to him. Explain what's happening. Our men can take care of the driver; if he doesn't resist, we won't harm him. We want to make friends, not enemies. We dump the driver and make off with Zola. Easy!"

"Where will we take him?" asked Gus.

"Here?" suggested Helena.

"No," said Yannis, "this is where they'll look for him. This is what they'd expect us to do. We need to do the unexpected."

"Then take the colonel into Corfu town," suggested Gus.

A light flashed the signal from the darkness above.

"Ready?" asked Yannis.

Gus nodded. "Ready."

They were dressed as Italian infantrymen, in light fawn-coloured jackets and baggy trousers held tightly around their calves by gaiters. Each wore a helmet and leather belt with ammunition pouches. Rifles were slung over their shoulders. Yannis wore the uniform of a corporal and Gus a private.

They saw the headlights of the approaching car, checked there was no traffic coming the other way, and then both men stepped into the road. As the car came up to them, Yannis waved a flashlight with a red filter over the lens.

The buff-coloured 508CM Coloniale four-seater slowed, then stopped. The soft top was up. Yannis walked up to the passenger door and Gus covered the driver's side. Both windows were wound down.

"Papers," said Yannis in the best Italian he could muster, shining the light into Zola's eyes. "Oh! Sorry, Colonel," he said, feigning surprise.

"No problem, Corporal," said Zola. "I'm pleased by your devotion to duty."

Taking the colonel completely by surprise, Yannis swung open the passenger door, grabbed him by the arm and dragged him out. Gus opened the other door and yanked out the driver. The sound of this commotion was a signal to Dimitri and Nikos, hiding in the trees. Nikos took care of the driver, knocking him unconscious, binding and gagging him, then dumping him in the trees. Dimitri removed Zola's jacket, then bundled him into the back seat of the car, a stiletto blade thrust at his throat. Nikos climbed in to sit on the other side of the colonel.

Gus was in the driver's seat, ready to go. Yannis wore Zola's jacket, the colonel's rank insignia on it, and forage cap. He climbed into the passenger seat beside Gus.

"Go, go!"

Gus put the Coloniale into gear and turned around in the road. The engine roared as they moved off, picking up speed.

"Not too quickly," warned Yannis. "Drive at about the pace a staff car would normally travel."

Gus slowed down a little and spoke to Zola. "Colonel Zola, I am Flying Officer Gus Beaumont, an officer of His Majesty's armed forces. Beside me is a captain of the Greek Army. You are now a prisoner of war under our protection. Do you understand?"

"I understand, Officer Beaumont. What are you going to do with me?"

"If you give us no trouble, you will be kept safe and, hopefully, within a few days you'll be back in your residence. If you try to escape, or worse, attempt to raise the alarm, then I can take no responsibility for what might happen."

"I offer you my parole and give you my word that I will not attempt to escape."

"I accept," said Gus. "Have your man ease off," he told Yannis.

Yannis turned to nod at Dimitri, who moved the blade a half inch away from Zola's throat but kept his eyes firmly on the Italian. Gus drove them back towards Corfu town, where there was an Italian checkpoint. Cool nerves, a frightened Colonel Zola and luck would be needed. A red light shone at them. The barrier was down.

Gus slowed the car. "You must be quiet, Colonel," he said.

Zola looked at Dimitri's knife. "Yes, I understand," he whispered.

As the car was about to stop, Yannis wound down the window. "Colonel Zola's car! Colonel Zola's car!" he shouted in Italian. The barrier was raised and soldiers saluted. Gus drove the car into the town.

They'd done it. Thirty minutes later, Colonel Zola was installed in a safehouse in the Old Town. He even had a lovely view out over the harbour.

Gus and Yannis put together a letter for Major Pepe Sartori. It explained that Zola was safe and would be handed over if the Greek doctor was released, unharmed, within two days. If not, then Zola would be kept prisoner in the mountains and eventually taken to England by the British, where he would spend the rest of the war as a prisoner.

The letter was then delivered in the night to Zola's headquarters, where Sartori had taken command.

Gus and Yannis, both of them unarmed, stood before Sartori at the agreed meeting place. Gus was in his RAF summer drill, spruced up as well as he and Helena could manage. Yannis was in the battle dress of the 10th Infantry Regiment. Sartori had arrived in a Fiat 3000 and Gus saw that another tank carried a lieutenant. Besides these, half a dozen Italian troops were standing in front of a lorry.

"It's just the two of you?" asked the English-speaking lieutenant, translating for Sartori.

"If you mean do we have an armoured convoy supporting us," said Gus, "then no. But our men are here. Are you Major Sartori?"

"I am."

"Well, Major, our men are concealed behind bushes and trees. You can't see them, but they have you and your soldiers covered. They're ready to open fire on our signal."

"Thank you for being truthful."

"It's as well we're honest, Major. I expect the same of you."

"Where is Colonel Zola?" asked Sartori.

"Safe."

"I asked where he is."

"Now, that would be telling," butted in Yannis.

"We need to discuss Colonel Zola's release, not his whereabouts," said Gus, impatiently. "We're prepared to exchange him for Doctor Andreas Nicolaides, who was arrested last week."

"You speak for these partisans, Flying Officer Beaumont?"

"Their commander is a Greek army officer, as you can see. My country is allied with Greece. We speak as one."

"What are your terms?" asked Sartori.

"No terms. A straightforward exchange of prisoners. Bring Doctor Nicolaides here this time tomorrow and we will bring the colonel. Colonel Zola has given me his parole and I have accepted. He will not try to escape in the meantime and will do nothing to hamper the exchange. Here is a note from him."

Gus handed Sartori the piece of paper on which Zola had written a brief message. "Tell me, why the interest in this old man, this Doctor Nicolaides?"

"The people of Gouvia need him," said Yannis. "He is a good doctor."

"And he will go back there, go back to practise again?"

"Yes," said Gus.

"What if we re-arrest him?"

"My men will not be so gentle with Colonel Zola next time," said Yannis. "Nor you, Major Sartori. If we think you're behind the re-arrest, we will kill you."

"Bring Zola here, tomorrow at 1300 hours," said Sartori.

"Good. We'll see you tomorrow. Oh, and Major," said Gus, "just so that you know, our men have been watching all this time. Lieutenant…"

Yannis raised his left hand. A shot rang out immediately and the flag flying from the aerial of Sartori's Fiat tank suddenly had a hole blown through it. The Italian soldiers reacted, instantly taking cover, removing the safety catches from their weapons and looking around. They saw nothing.

"Most of our men are hunters and shepherds," said Yannis. "They are very good shots."

"I can see that," growled Sartori.

The exchange took place the following day. It was without event. Zola, embarrassed by the whole affair, skulked back to his headquarters. His journey home along the Dimokratias was escorted by a Fiat 3000 tank and a truck full of soldiers.

There was no need for such caution. The partisans, Doctor Nicolaides amongst them, were camped high in the mountains to the east of the plain. They had ouzo, kleftiko and red wine. Afterwards, a bottle of tsipouro appeared. Nikos produced a strung musical instrument, which Gus thought similar to a guitar.

The music began slowly, a combination of notes strange to Gus's ears. Helena rose and began moving in time with the music. Then Yannis and Dimitri got up, one on each side of her, their arms outstretched, hands on each other's shoulders. They began moving in a circular direction, anti-clockwise. Other partisans joined them, including the few other women with the band. The old doctor got up, and Helena called to Gus, "Come on, join us. You can dance, can't you?"

"I can do a passable foxtrot," said Gus, "but I'm not sure about this."

He had no choice. Helena came away from the line of dancers, took him firmly by the hand and pulled him into the dance.

"We call this dance Perdika," said Helena, as they moved rhythmically to Nikos's strumming. "It's very similar to the Kalamatianós, danced all over Greece."

The music quickened. As the dancers moved to the music, they began to weave in and out of each other, their line creating circular patterns around the campfire. The dancing became faster. Gus was sweating. Faster they went, spinning and reeling around. Eventually they stopped and collapsed into grateful heaps around the fire, smiling, laughing and gasping for air.

Nikos, still strumming tunefully, began to sing in Greek.

"What is he saying?" asked Gus.

"It's a love story," said Helena. "I will try to translate for you:

My red apple, painted pomegranate,
why have you wilted me, sour one?
I come and go, but cannot find you.
I try your door, but it is locked.
Your windows are always lit, and I ask your door,
'Where has the lady gone?'
'My lady is not here, she's gone to find water at the wellspring, she's gone to fill her cup.'
Thank you, thank you."

"Beautiful," said Gus, gazing at Helena as she spoke.

"My translation may not be perfect."

"It really doesn't matter. I understand the meaning. Something lost. Somebody…"

The music stopped abruptly. Yannis rose and stood by the fire. Nikos started up again, a different tune this time. Gus listened as the partisans began clapping rhythmically with the music.

Yannis danced. He danced by the fire, around the fire and even in the fire. His movements were strong; he dived onto the ground as though doing gymnastic press-ups, then jumped high in the air, swinging his leg above the heads of those seated, missing them by less than an inch.

The final dance was performed by Helena with the old doctor. As she danced — gracefully, seductively, thought Gus — in front of the doctor, he clapped and moved from foot to foot. Suddenly he took the gold chain from around his neck and gave it to Gus. A ring from his finger went to Dimitri, a coin to one of the women. Then the old man removed his shirt and, to great applause, he threw it into the seated throng of partisans.

Afterwards Helena and Yannis sat by Gus. "What on earth was that all about?" he asked.

"Some say it is a symbol of man giving up his worldly treasures for the love of a beautiful woman," said Yannis.

"And others say it's an old man willing to pay for the charms of a young woman," offered Helena. "You may choose which you prefer."

Whatever the translation of the song or interpretation of the dance, for Gus it had been a wonderful evening to end the best of days. Gus, Helena, Yannis and his father finished the night with large glasses of Metaxa.

CHAPTER 12

It proved easy enough to determine that the Bredas were re-armed and re-fuelled immediately after returning from a sortie.

"Early morning seems the best time, then," offered Gus. "Generally, the air crews have their breakfast at eight and make it last a good hour. Your engineer and I can run over to the leading aircraft, start her up, then get the thing airborne as quick as we can. Hopefully I can hit the other pair with machine guns, drop bombs on the runway, then make my escape down to Crete. What about the guards?"

"I'll have men surround them," replied Yannis. "I assume they'll spring into action once they spot you or hear the engine start up. We'll open fire as soon as they move. Once our man is back with us, we'll get out quickly and leave it to you. Will the Italians try to intercept you afterwards?"

"They're likely to report it by radio and call in a fighter or two to try to get me."

"They won't. We'll hit the radio control room with a grenade attack."

"Sounds risky."

"Maybe."

"Then don't do it on my account. I'll disappear to the east at low level, over towards the mainland, and I'll make sure they see me go that way. They won't see when I turn south; I doubt they'd ever guess that's the direction I'll be heading in. They won't know I'm English until Sartori works it out. I'll take my chance, Yannis."

"You are a brave man," said the Greek.

"So are you. You and your men are running a big risk, fighting the Italians the way you do…"

"And women, Bouncer."

"Of course. If they ever catch you…"

"I know."

"Why do you do it?" Gus asked.

"Greece is my country. This is my island. I was born and bred in Gouvia and I'll fight to get it back."

"That's how my cousin Staś feels. He's Polish and his country has been divided between the Nazis and the Russians. He fights in the skies above England for a free Poland."

"That's a similar situation. Nationalism. But there's more to it than nationalism…"

Gus waited for him to carry on. Helena arrived with coffee.

"He means we're communists," she said.

"Yes," said Yannis. "Our group, the Communist Party of Greece, dominates the resistance here on Corfu. But we are working with other left-wing parties to form a National Liberation Front."

"What other parties?"

"The Socialists, the Agricultural Party and the People's Party."

"And what will you do once the Italians have been defeated?" asked Gus.

"Fight the Germans," said Helena, who had sat down with them.

"You know what I mean."

"We'll carry on fighting for socialism and a communist Greece," said Yannis. Helena nodded her support.

Gus was gazing up at three dots in the sky; they were becoming larger and taking on the shape of birds. The he realised what they were and at the same time heard the droning noise of the engines. It must be the Bredas. He pointed to them and shouted, "We're under attack! Yannis, get your men under cover!"

The Greeks couldn't be calmed. Angered and affronted by an attack on their base, they had already taken up their rifles and started shooting at the Italian planes. Gus took Helena by the arm and began running towards a group of rocks at the edge of some trees. Together they dived for cover.

"It's no use trying to shoot them down like that," he said urgently. "It never works. Better to take cover, live to fight another day. Tell them, Helena, tell them to take cover — those damned planes have machine guns as well as bombs!"

Helena shouted, ordering the andarte to take cover. Some of them did, crouching behind rocks or buildings and shooting from there.

"Not the buildings!" shouted Gus. "Get them away. That's where the pilots will aim their bombs." Helena translated and soon most of the fighters were in some sort of cover away from the small group of huts.

The Bredas were losing height; Gus watched as the flaps altered the shape of their wings for a low-level approach. They came in line, one aeroplane behind the other aiming directly at the buildings. The first Breda dropped its bombs and an explosion quickly followed; then the second came in and dropped its load into the plume of smoke and dust created by the first. Gus wasn't sure, but he thought the third plane hadn't released its bomb load as the three aircraft screamed overhead.

Gus looked at the few huts; surprisingly, it didn't look as though too much damage had been done. Not that it mattered, the Italians knew where they were and Yannis would have to move his men.

"Stay down!" shouted Gus as the Greeks rose. "They'll turn and come back for another attack. Find cover!" Helena translated and the men looked skywards. Sure enough, there were the bombers, turning and preparing for another low attack into the wind.

It'll be machine guns this time, maybe more bombs, thought Gus. *They know we don't have anti-aircraft capacity.* "Tell them to stay under cover, Helena."

But as the three planes swooped in, there was Yannis cursing and shouting at them. He stood in the centre of the camp, pointing his Lee-Enfield at the leading aircraft. The leading Breda opened fire with all four of its machine guns, flame and bullets spitting from them, raising dust from the ground around Yannis. Still he stood there, aiming at the leading Italian plane.

Yannis fired. The aeroplane flew overhead, unscathed. Then he fell to the ground, hit by the bullets from the second Breda.

Helena jumped up and ran to him. "No!" shouted Gus, as he saw the third aircraft lining up for its own strafing run. Helena ignored him and ran towards Yannis. Gus jumped up and sprinted after her. They grabbed an arm each, struggled to drag Yannis back towards the trees. Once in the safety of the woodland, Helena talked gently, lovingly to Yannis, stroking his blood-splattered head. She looked at Gus. "He's dead."

"I'm so sorry." There was nothing more he could say.

The andarte dug a grave for their leader. Helena, Doctor Nicolaides, Gus and the others stood around the grave and spoke over it. As they walked back to the damaged huts to gather their belongings and what was left of the ammunition, Helena said, "This is what I saw in the coffee grounds. You and me standing over Yannis' grave."

Later that evening Gus sat with Helan beside the fire. The old doctor and the rest of the andarte were on the far side, some distance away from them.

"I'm sorry to talk to you this way, about Yannis. But I can't talk to the others."

"It's all right, Helena, I understand. I can listen."

"I've known Yannis since we were teenagers. Although I came from St Stephanos and he from Gouvia, after basic school we'd both been educated in Corfu town. We hit it off straight away. Yannis told me he was enticed first by my good looks and later, more strongly, by my intelligence and strength of character. I admired him for his passion. Passion for medicine, for Greece, for socialism. And for his sense of humour, you never had a chance to see that."

"No."

"In Corfu town, without our parents or relatives to chaperone us, we found it easy to meet and go for strolls along the Liston or around the citadel. In the holidays we had to be more inventive to create opportunities. Once, I remember, it was a blisteringly hot summer day. We made excuses and met at Ypsos bay, where we weren't known. I brought some food and Yannis had taken a half bottle of white wine from his father's kitchen. We sat and talked for ages, then I jumped to my feet. I said we should go for a swim. 'But we don't have swimming costumes,' he complained. I told him that there was nobody else here, and we could strip down to our underclothes behind a bush. Then I went and did so. 'Don't look!' I shouted to him, and I made him let me get into the water first. He said he wouldn't look, but I didn't believe him. I'm sure he peeked a little.

"I ran and splashed into the sea, whimpering at first as the cold water washed over my skin. Yannis turned around and looked at me. 'Come on!' I shouted. It was so lovely in the sea. Yannis stripped quickly behind the bush and walked onto the beach. The pebbles poked into his feet, making him walk awkwardly as he came towards the water to join me. I'm sure he saw my eyes surveying his body."

"When was that?"

"Must have been five years ago. Then, when the Italians arrived on the island, he asked me if I would help. 'Of course, I'll help,' I told him. 'But don't expect me just to do women's work.' I reminded Yannis that I knew these coastlines and these mountains just as well as he did. I told him I could learn how to shoot a rifle and fight alongside him and the other men." She turned to Gus, her brown eyes full of tears. "Then Yannis told me he loved me and asked if, after this blasted war, I would marry him. I told him yes. Yes, I would."

PART THREE: ESCAPING 1941

CHAPTER 13

The andarte were on the Italians' airbase near Gouvia, ready for Gus to steal an aeroplane. The engineer assisting them, predictably called Spiros, spoke no English. Helena had taken over leadership of the andarte group and had briefed the man, translating Gus's instructions. Gus thought he looked capable, trustworthy. It was seven-thirty, nearly time to get into action. All they needed was a signal to tell them Helena and the andarte were in position and ready.

Young Spiros was very good at impersonating bird calls, a skill he'd developed in his youth — something to pass the time in those hours spent at sea or lazing in the shade on a sunny afternoon. Helena sent a runner to tell him that the guardroom was surrounded. Spiros made ready to give the call.

Gus heard the short, rhythmical scream of a Scops owl. The same sound was repeated exactly ten seconds later. This was it. Gus glanced around. Nobody was about apart from a lone soldier walking from one block of wooden buildings to another. The man had his back to them and didn't seem to have noticed Gus and Spiros the engineer. He tapped his companion on the shoulder and gave him a thumbs-up. Then the pair sprinted across the grass to the leading Breda Ba-65. Gus quickly clambered into the cockpit and surveyed the controls, making sense of them: joystick, throttle. He played with some controls, watching how the rudder and flaps responded. Where was the fuel cut-off? There it was.

Spiros stood by the prop awaiting orders. Gus looked around again. The lone Italian soldier had disappeared into a low building, possibly the mess. He was probably tucking into a nice breakfast, which Gus was about to interrupt. He gave a thumbs-up again and Spiros heaved on a propeller blade. Nothing. He tried again. There was a puff of smoke, but the engine still didn't catch. Spiros got ready for a third try, putting all of his substantial weight and strength into the task. This time the powerful Fiat eighteen-cylinder, twin-row radial engine burst into life.

Gus ordered chocks away and opened the throttle, taxiing quickly onto the grassy strip. The guardroom door flew open. Two Italian soldiers rushed out to see the Breda moving away. Running towards them was Spiros the engineer. One of the soldiers raised his rifle and took aim at the sprinting partisan.

Helena's andarte opened fire and both Italians fell down dead as the Ba-65 soared into the air. The Breda gained height. Gus turned it around in a tight arc so that it was facing the other two Ba-65s on the ground. He approached at low level and in a straight line; when he was fifty feet short of the first aeroplane, Gus opened fire with all four forward-facing machine guns, two 12.7mm guns and two 7.7mm. The first Breda shattered to pieces under the heavy blast of machine-gun fire as Gus switched his aim to the second. As Gus flew away, he saw in his rear-view mirror that both the grounded aircraft were now in flames.

The Italian base had no anti-aircraft guns, as clearly nobody had anticipated an attack from the skies. But Major Sartori's force did have a couple of Fiat-Revelli Modello 35 8mm machine guns, which the sergeant now sprinted towards to get into action. He needn't have bothered. Though the belt-fed, air-cooled machine guns were lighter than their predecessor, they were tripod-mounted and needed a crew of three to operate. There was no way the Italians would get them into use in time.

Gus gained some height, turned again and flew towards the runway. It was the only straight and level strip of land for miles around, and if he could put a couple of bomb craters onto it, it would take the Italians months to put right the damage. He reached for what he thought was the bomb release control. Keeping his eyes on the runway, Gus straightened up then levelled off.

As the Breda flew towards the grassy runway strip, Gus spotted some soldiers trying to assemble a machine gun. It was going to damage either him or Helena's andarte. He altered course slightly and let loose the Breda's remaining ammo, killing the gun crew instantly. Then he straightened, lined up the runway below him, and pressed the bomb release control. A stick of bombs tumbled from the aircraft. As he took up a due east course, Gus saw the destruction on the ground, and waggled the wings of the Breda in a final farewell to Helena Papachristodoulopoulos and the andarte of Corfu.

CHAPTER 14

Once out of sight of the island, Gus had checked his compass and put the Breda on a course that would take him to Crete. From a map loaned to him by the andarte, he worked out that Crete was over two hundred miles away, so he slowed the Breda to a gentle three hundred kilometres per hour to conserve fuel. He tried to relax. He had little to worry about above the Ionian Sea. Any Italian or German fighters spotting him might think it an odd sight but were unlikely to open fire on him. The closer he came to Crete, however, the more likely he was to be bounced by the RAF.

After about three-quarters of an hour, Gus spotted two Gloster Gladiators circling above him. *Time to act*, he thought, and quickly flung back the cockpit canopy and let loose the white sheet Helena had provided for him. He'd already tied one corner of it firmly onto a sturdy piece of cockpit. They'd thought about writing 'English' on it in large letters, but decided it wouldn't be readable. Keep it simple, he'd said to the Greeks. A plain white sheet it was.

He watched as one of the Gladiators came up alongside, its wingman circling above. As the pilot opened the cockpit canopy, Gus waved and pointed to the Flying Officer stripes on the cuffs of his RAF tunic. The pilot gave the thumbs-up. He was safe.

The Gladiator biplanes flew, one ahead and one behind him, to the island of Crete, providing Gus with his first ever escort. He landed the Breda heavily on the strip at RAF Maleme then followed the leading Gladiator as it taxied over to its depot. The ground crew stared as Gus pulled the Breda up beside the

British plane, shut off the fuel supply to the engine and clambered down from the cockpit. The Gladiator pilots and ground crew came over to him. Some, he noticed, were armed with rifles. He raised both arms. "It's all right," he announced, "We're on the same side. Thank God I'm back with Brits, if not home, exactly!"

"Mind me asking who the bloody hell you are?" asked one of the British pilots.

"Not at all. Flying Officer Gus Beaumont. I had the misfortune to crash-land a Blenheim on Corfu a few weeks ago. Pinched that Italian kite and now I'm here. I'd better report to my squadron, assuming they're here? A bomber squadron, 732. Have you come across them?"

"I think you'd better report to our squadron leader first, if you don't mind," said the pilot, smiling and offering his hand. "I'm Roger Costello, by the way. Fellows in the mess call me Dodger. Pleased to meet you."

Gus happily shook hands. "Call me Bouncer," he said.

Costello led Gus away to the office of Squadron Leader Ernie Hosking, whose Gladiators had intercepted and escorted him. Explaining to Hosking much of his adventures on Corfu, Gus asked after the whereabouts of his squadron.

"Bit of bad news there, old boy," said Hosking. "They've been through here recently. But they aren't here any longer, I'm afraid. The squadron suffered badly when they were attacked by Bf-109s near Florina in the Monastir Gap. Seven of their Blenheims were shot down. The German advance forced them back, first to Agrinion and then to Tatoi, from where the squadron was evacuated through Crete."

"Where are they now, sir?"

"Egypt, to the best of my knowledge. At least, that's where they were sent from here."

"Then I'd better get back to them."

"Could do with some help here, actually, if you can wait a few days. Lost a few pilots recently. Flown Gladiators before, have you?"

"No, sir. I've flown Spits and Hurricanes, though."

"80 Squadron was re-equipped with Hurricanes in February, but we're still waiting. The Glads are pretty useful kites. The boys in 33 Squadron have shot down twenty or so Italians, mostly in Glads. Look, I'm desperate and I don't mind saying so. Could you agree to stay a while and give us a hand? At least until you contact your squadron?"

"Yes, sir, I suppose I can. But may I try to get a message to my own unit?"

"Oh, good show! Of course, you can get a message sent. We'll get something off by radio. We have regular flights out that carry mail as well. Over there —" Hosking pointed to a spare desk — "are some letter-writing materials. Off you go. Write to as many people as you like — the next post run is tomorrow morning. I'll get you some tea, or would you like something stronger?"

"Tea will be fine, thanks, and, er..." Gus pulled something from the small kitbag he'd carried in the Breda. "Please accept this as a thank-you for your reception committee. I mean the escort fighters." He handed over a couple of bottles of ouzo. "A gift from the kind people of Corfu, sir!"

As Squadron Leader Hosking sorted out refreshments, Gus scribbled two brief letters. The first was to his squadron.

To the Officer Commanding 732 Squadron RAF
10th May 1941

Dear Sir,

As you know, on 15th April I took off from RAF Menidi to attack the Italians in Vlorë. Alongside me were Flying Officer Linton and Flight Sergeant Apps. After successfully dropping our bombs we were intercepted by Italian fighters and the Blenheim suffered damage, both engines cutting out over the sea by Corfu. I successfully crash-landed and the three of us were picked up by the Corfu Resistance.

I am sad to report that Flying Officer Linton was badly injured and handed over to the Italians for medical treatment. I assume he is now a POW. Flight Sergeant Apps was taken by boat towards Crete, but I have heard nothing of him since he left Corfu (this would be approximately 20th or 21st April). I was unable to accompany Sergeant Apps as I had picked up some illness whilst on Corfu.

Upon recovery, I stole an Italian aeroplane and flew directly to Crete, where the Resistance assured me the British had 'dug in'. In the process of executing my escape, I destroyed two Italian Ba-65 bombers and shot up some of their ground forces, inflicting much damage on a runway and base near Gouvia.

I landed on Crete today, hoping to make contact with the squadron, but have been advised of your re-deployment to Egypt. I have been requested to stay on and give assistance to a fighter squadron here in Crete. In the circumstances, I have decided to do this whilst awaiting the opportunity of getting to Egypt or receiving alternative orders.

Flying Officer G. Beaumont

The second letter was to Sir Alexander Peacock. Gus needed to be careful. Some officious junior might be into censoring officers' letters, though he doubted it.

10th May 1941

Dear Uncle Alex,

I am safely back from a brief jaunt to the delightful island of Corfu. The ouzo there is very good, sadly not the white wine. Everything on Corfu is red — only red. More details once I'm in Blighty.

Yours Aye, your devoted nephew, Gustaw.

Group Captain George Beamish was an uncompromising officer and a tough man. Hailing from Dunmanway in County Cork, the birthplace of Sam McGuire, Beamish preferred rugby to Gaelic football. He was a fine player and had capped twenty-five times for Ireland and had been selected for the 1930 British Lions tour to New Zealand and Australia.

Beamish was considering the situation. Bluntly, it had been a shambles so far.

The group captain had been appointed Senior Air Officer, Crete, in April, taking over from an inadequately briefed flight lieutenant. His initial orders were to cover the evacuation of twenty-five thousand British and Dominion troops to the island, and to help with this, Beamish was ordered to prepare for the arrival of two Bristol Blenheim bomber squadrons from Egypt and the remaining fighter aircraft from Greece.

So far so good. These squadrons had arrived, along with some odds-and-sods, including a flying officer who had arrived in a captured Italian bomber and was now attached to a Gladiator squadron. But the idea of now moving this Allied force to the Middle East and reinforcing Greece with fresh troops from Egypt was utter nonsense. The Germans were hitting Crete with everything they had.

Beamish realised that the action he was overseeing was turning out to be the defence of Crete. If he was unable to convince the army commander of the need to defeat the German invaders from the air and get substantial reinforcements, the island would certainly fall.

Gus soon found the Gladiator an easy and comfortable aeroplane to fly. Dodger Costello sat him in the cockpit and went over the controls with him. The main instruments were arranged in the standard 'T' layout, with a 'spade grip' control column housing a brake lever and buttons for radio and guns. The pilot seat was surrounded by exposed metal tubes, providing mounting points for the various other control levers. Gus found the adjustable seat and rudder pedals made it easy to find a comfortable position. His feet were supported below the rudder pedals on two metal trays. There was no cockpit floor as such.

"Better not drop anything down there," advised Costello. "It'll disappear into the bowels of the Glad, never to be seen again."

"Anything I need to know about the kite?"

"She's a pleasure to fly," said Costello, "but be easy with the throttle. Slam it open and you might cause the carburettor accelerator pump to flood the engine. It can soon cause a stoppage. The Glad isn't an aircraft to relax in during landing, though. You need about sixty-five knots on final approach for a tail down, three-pointer. Forward vision is poor, but you mustn't let her swing; it can quickly get out of hand. Get the stick hard back to get some weight on the tailwheel. It's not really that difficult. You've flown Hurries, right?"

"Yes, and Spitfires."

"You lucky bugger. Well, just remember, the Glad isn't as quick and doesn't pack the same punch. You've only got four Brownings."

"I'll make sure I get close, then," replied Gus.

It was time for his first flight. After some basic cockpit checks, including checking the operation of the hydraulic flaps and priming the engine with the Ki-Gass hand pump, Gus was ready to start. With the brakes set, external power connected and chocks in position Gus switched on the two main magnetos along with the third starting magneto. He had the throttle set only about an eighth open, as Costello advised, and the Ki-Gass pump ready for another shot to help the engine should it fail to catch. He signalled the ground crew and the electric starter turned over the big Bristol Mercury IX, a powerful nine-cylinder air-cooled radial engine. Turning slowly at first, the engine caught and roared to life, smoke billowing from the exhaust.

Gus lined up the Gladiator for take-off. He opened the throttle slowly and the big radial began to rumble as the aircraft slowly started to accelerate. The view directly forward was non-existent as the tailwheel of the plane was still on the ground, but Gus had the starboard side panel of the cockpit lowered so was able to lean out for a better view forward whilst taxiing. He avoided any swing with a dab of brake. The stick was hard back to keep weight on the tailwheel and keep her running straight. As the biplane gathered speed, Gus eased the stick forward and pushed the throttle further forward. The speed increased and, as the rudder became effective, Gus eased the control column further forward to raise the tail. Now he had a much better view ahead. At about sixty knots Gus felt the Gladiator lift off and he was airborne.

It was a beautiful late summer's day and Gus flew out towards the Mediterranean Sea. He found the biplane to be a real pilot's aircraft: manoeuvrable, with fairly light, well-harmonised controls. Pity, really, that it was completely outclassed by the Bfe-109s, 110s and even the latest Italian fighters. In truth, the Glads were obsolete.

Early next morning, three Gladiators were scrambled. Gus and Pilot Officer Ray Whitney were ordered up to meet the attackers, led by Dodger Costello. As they gained sufficient height, Gus saw scores of aircraft heading for Heraklion.

"Tally-ho!" called Costello, and down they swept.

There were so many German aircraft that the Gladiators were soon split up. Gus saw nine Heinkel He-111s turning in a wide circle south of the island without any obvious fighter escort. He thought they may have dropped their bombs and were preparing to head back to mainland Greece. Cutting across the circle, he gave chase, quickly gaining on one of the twin-engined He-111s. He had the sun behind him, which would make it difficult for the rear-gunner to see. Gus swept down and closed in on the German. *Closer, closer, remember what Staś and the Poles advised.* He closed to point-blank range and opened fire on the Heinkel. Smoke appeared from its port engine. The bomber peeled off, away from its unit.

Gus homed in on a second He-111. This time he didn't have surprise or the sun on his side. Gunfire spat from the rear guns of the German bomber. He got closer, then opened fire and discharged the remainder of his ammunition. The bomber's starboard engine burst into flames. His ammo spent, Gus returned to base to find Costello already there. Ray Whitney, sadly, never came back from that sortie.

Five hours later the Gladiators were scrambled again, Gus and Costello going up to intercept a lone Ju-88 which was obviously reconnoitring the result of the morning raid on Heraklion. They gained height. Costello went in first, leaving Gus to look out for fighters. Costello sprayed bullets at the German's tail but didn't appear to have done any significant damage. Meanwhile, the Nazi pilot turned and headed north with Gus in pursuit. Gus got within range and opened fire. Smoke emerged from the port wing and both Gus and Costello watched as the crew jumped from the wounded plane, their parachutes opening and billowing in the air.

That night Gus, close to collapse, relaxed, if it could be called that, over a Scotch in the mess. He had flown five sorties during the day. The final one had been the worst. Just before dusk that fifth raid had come in and the Gladiators were once again scrambled — Stukas this time. Gus attacked two Ju-87s without result. Suddenly, he was bounced by two escorting Bf-109s. The leading German fighter had blasted off hundreds of rounds at Gus, but at long range. No damage was done. Gus went into a steep dive. A Gladiator couldn't outrun a modern German fighter, but with a good pilot in the cockpit, he thought it could outmanoeuvre a Bf-109. He remembered his pre-war training and the 180-degree flat turn he'd done in a Tiger Moth, astonishing his instructors. Very few aircraft could accomplish it, as it needed an incredibly low stalling speed. The Moth was ideal. How about a Glad? Maybe … maybe not. But then, Gus didn't need as much as a 180-degree turn — less would do, and those Messerschmitts were gaining on him. He'd descended to a dangerously low level and pulled up the nose to slow the Glad. The biplane's undercarriage was almost touching the treetops. A 109 fired again and Gus saw tracer bullets ahead of him. Slowly, calmly, and with a lot of rudder, the Gladiator turned to starboard like a skater pirouetting on ice. The German fighters screamed by and soared away to the north. With sweat around his face mask and his heart thumping, Gus had decided to chase off any remaining Stukas before returning to base.

He gained height, looked around and spotted a Junkers dive-bomber below him, set up nicely for a good swoop out of the setting sun. He dived on the unsuspecting Ju-87, throttling back, his height advantage being so great. Gus closed on the Stuka, closer, closer… The German rear gunner opened fire, bullets crashing into the Gladiator. Gus opened fire. The Stuka pilot put his own aircraft into a dive, but Gus stuck to him as he'd been taught by the Poles, ignoring intermittent fire from the rear gunner. They were getting very close to the ground. Then, at around twelve-hundred feet, the Stuka pulled out of the dive and started to climb. This shortened the range and Gus gave him another burst from the Gladiator's nose-mounted machine guns. The German returned to a port dive, trying desperately to get away from Gus's bullets. They were approaching the coast on the easternmost tip of the island, the Stuka still diving. Gus had had enough. He pulled out of the dive and swerved to starboard as the Stuka crashed into the cliffs, exploding into flame and smoke. He looked at his fuel gauge. Time to return to base.

On 19th May 1941, Gus received replies to the letters he'd sent nine days earlier. Both were curt. The first was from 732 Squadron:

Flying Officer Beaumont is to report to his squadron at RAF Aqir at the earliest possible opportunity.

The second was from Peacock. It read:

Dear Gustaw,

I have some business for you in Malta. Expect new posting, but perhaps not very soon.

"Where's RAF Aqir, Dodger?"

"Aqir? I think it's in Palestine. There's a map here, somewhere." He searched for the map of the southern Mediterranean. "Yes, here we are. RAF Aqir. It's west of Jerusalem."

Gus later heard that the day after he left Crete for Aqir, Group Captain Beamish ordered all RAF squadrons on Crete to withdraw to Egypt. The next day, German paratroopers fell from the blue skies above Crete. Jumping from dozens of Junkers Ju-52 aircraft, the paratroopers landed near RAF Maleme. There was fighting all day as the Germans were held by New Zealanders. Group captain Beamish remained on Crete to assist General Freyberg, both men escaping the island later aboard a Short Sunderland flying boat.

CHAPTER 15

"Good news, men," said Squadron Leader Percy Lambert, a wide grin supporting his handlebar moustache. "We may have lost Crete, indeed, lost Greece, but every cloud has a silver lining and you, my merry men, have a spot of leave coming up."

A tired-looking collection of pilot officers, flying officers and the odd flight lieutenant cheered.

Gus had rejoined 732 squadron only the previous day. He, Dodger Costello, and the rest of the squadron had flown their Gladiators over from Crete to Egypt. Gus made his way to Aqir by hitching a lift in an Avro Anson. Once there, he found only the aeroplanes and flight crews of the squadron. They'd outrun their ground crews and admin staff and these 'left-behinds' were being shipped across the Mediterranean. Everyone was worried about their fate. A spot of leave seemed a very good idea.

"What will you do?" asked his friend, Freddie Eaton.

"Have a look around the country. Four days is enough to get about a bit."

"Rather!" said Freddie. "I fancy Cairo — I hear there's a few spiffing nightclubs there. Up for it?"

"No thanks. As a matter of fact, I have relatives living close by. Thought I might visit and get them to take me sightseeing, Jerusalem, Bethlehem, maybe Nazareth — if it's not too far away. Fancy joining me?"

"No! No offence, old boy, but the nightlife in Cairo seems an awful lot livelier, if you don't mind me saying so."

Freddie Eaton and two other officers flew a Blenheim to Cairo. The squadron never found out if they had a spiffing time in the bars there, as the aircraft crashed in the desert on the return trip, the wreckage discovered weeks later by a long-range desert patrol. Their bodies were never found.

Gus hitched a lift from Aqir to the outskirts of the Rehovot Yishuv. He found his uncle simply by walking around asking for Theodore Rosen.

"Gustaw, my boy!" said Uncle Theodore. "So good to see you, and thank you for looking me up. What a surprise! My goodness, how long has it been? I don't expect you actually remember, do you?"

"No, I'm afraid not, Uncle," said Gus.

"Well, well. No matter. I was so very sorry to hear of your father's death. A couple of years ago, wasn't it? Sad news, so sad. And tell me, Gustaw, how is your mother?"

"She's doing all right, Uncle. She gets rather depressed sometimes, but she's coping."

"Any news of the others?"

"Cousin Stanislaw — Staś — is doing well. He's in England with a Polish fighter squadron. He did very well in the Battle of Britain."

"Good, good. Let's hope he survives this mess. Let's hope we all do. Now, what shall we do with you for a couple of days? Any ideas?"

"I'll leave it to you, Uncle."

"Tomorrow, I thought we might go to Ramleh. There is a British war cemetery there. Soldiers from the Great War and some soldiers, police and airmen who have died here during the Mandate. I thought you might be interested?"

"Yes, of course."

Then we could visit Jerusalem, if you like. Bethlehem. I know you Beaumonts are secular Judaeo-Christians, but you, young man, have always been interested in history. Am I correct?"

"Yes. And I'd be fascinated, Uncle."

"We might even get to Hebron. I'd like you to see the Tomb of the Patriarchs. You've heard of it?"

"A little," said Gus, his lack of conviction obvious to his uncle.

"It's all there in the Book of Genesis," said Theodore. "Abraham purchased a plot in the Land of Canaan from Ephron the Hittite. He bought it for use as a burial plot. Three patriarchs, Abraham, Isaac and Jakob are buried there along with their wives, the matriarchs: Sarah, Rebekah and Leah."

"I'm sure."

"Ah yes, but I expect you see the Bible as a work of myth rather than history?"

"Most historians believe the Abraham-Isaac-Jacob narrative to be primarily mythological," said Gus.

"But still worth a visit?"

"Definitely worth a visit. Yes, please."

"We may not see the tomb itself."

"Why not?"

"It lies inside the Ibrahimi Mosque. Perhaps they will let you in, we'll see. But not me. Things are difficult between the Muslims and Jews in Hebron. In fact, there are few Jews in Hebron these days."

"Why is that?"

"After the violence there in 1929, all Hebron's Jews were evacuated by the British authorities. Many returned after a few years, but almost all were displaced again at the outbreak of the 1936–39 rising."

"What happened in 1929?"

"There were rumours that Jews were planning to seize control of the Temple Mount in Jerusalem. Some of the Arabs were incited by this and attacked the Jews. About seventy Jews and some Arabs were killed in the fighting. Jewish homes were pillaged. Synagogues ransacked."

"Bad news everywhere."

"Yes. But it's also worth remembering that many of the Jews who survived were hidden by local Arab families."

Uncle Theodore had borrowed a car, a maroon-coloured Morris. Gus drove, his uncle giving directions. It took them thirty minutes to drive from Rehovot to the Commonwealth War Graves Commission cemetery in Ramleh. There were thousands of graves. The two men strolled together in the morning sunshine, stopping occasionally to consider the details etched into white stone.

"Look at this one, Uncle," said Gus, pointing to a gravestone. "Interesting name for an Englishman fighting a war against Germany."

Theodore examined the inscription. "Private D. German. The Devonshire Regiment," he read out loud. "Died 9th April 1918 aged nineteen. Such a waste."

Gus nodded as they walked on.

"The British were fighting against the Turks here in Palestine."

"Yes," said Gus, "but look." He pointed to another grave, the inscription in German. "Unteroffizier H. Vesper. Fliegerabt 301. Died at the end of August 1918."

"*Unteroffizier* — that means sergeant, yes?" asked Uncle Theodore. "But *Fliegerabt* 301, what's that? My German isn't that good, I'm afraid."

"Possibly an abbreviation. Feldflieger Abteilung, perhaps? Aviation section, something like that?"

"Makes sense," said Theodore. "The German air force was supporting the ground troops of their Turkish ally. Over there —" he pointed to a line of graves near the entrance to the cemetery — "are the graves of English police who have been killed in conflict here."

"What were they doing here?" asked Gus.

"They'd say they were keeping the peace between Arabs and Jews."

"What would you say, Uncle?"

"I'd say they were protecting British interests. And, if I'm truthful, I wish the English would go away and leave us be. We can sort out things peaceably between ourselves."

From Ramleh, Gus drove them into the Latrun hilltops. Uncle Theodore wanted him to see the Trappist Monastery at Neve Shalom. They climbed a hill and gazed over the Ayalon Valley.

"The promised land," said Theodore. "There it is, Gustaw."

The two men gazed at the immense countryside spread before them. From the Latrun hills looking west they could see a flat, brown landscape stretching to the coast.

"It's hardly a land of milk and honey, is it? It looks harsh to me."

"It needs work. But the climate is good, and God provides water. We can grow all the food we need here. We can live good, wholesome, fulfilled lives in this land."

Gus pointed to a large plant with spiked leaves and a thistle-like flowerhead, clinging to the sparse earth on the hilltop.

"I never realised plants like these grew here, Uncle," said Gus, examining it. "Looks like a teasel or something. I think of thistles being Scottish. What is it?"

"I'm not sure. I don't know it in Polish anyway. A cardoon in English, I think. Sorry, I don't know for sure what it's called. I'm not good with plants."

"Cardoon? That even sounds Scottish."

"There are hundreds of them around here, thousands. That's a small one; some grow as tall as a man. I think there may be an edible version."

"Edible version? Is that an artichoke?"

"Yes, that's it."

"You know the story of artichokes, don't you, Uncle?"

"No. Tell me."

"Well, according to the Greek myths, the artichoke originated after the philandering god Zeus became smitten by a beautiful young woman named Cynara. Zeus used his powers to turn Cynara into a goddess so that she could live near him and keep him entertained; this was while his wife Hera was away."

"Something tells me this isn't going to end well," suggested Theodore.

"Cynara became homesick, so she sidled off back to earth to visit her family. Zeus was so enraged by her betrayal that he banished her from Mount Olympus for good and turned her into an artichoke."

Theodore smiled. "I've brought us a picnic. No artichokes, I'm afraid. It's in the car. Come on, let's eat."

Lunch was delicious. They ate falafels, sliced and pushed into unleavened bread, flavoured by yoghurt and a spicy sauce. There was beer to drink.

"I admire our Muslim friends for their abstinence," said Theodore, "but I'm afraid it's not for me. You know that hops came to Europe from this part of the world, the Levant?"

"Yes, I knew that."

Afterwards they drove onwards to Jerusalem. Theodore directed them to the Jewish Quarter and eventually to the house of his friend Dawid Joselewicz. Theodore knocked on the door and a young man answered.

"Good afternoon, my son," said Theodore. "I am a friend of the late master of this house and his brother, Mordechai. My commiserations to all the Joselewicz family on the untimely deaths last year of those two eminent gentlemen. We are in need of accommodation for the night."

"Yes, sir, you are welcome," said the young man, "but at the moment there are a lot of us here. It's a bit noisy."

"No problem; we are all Jews. We can join you."

Gus followed Theodore into the main room of the small house, where a group of five men sat around. Theodore immediately recognised one of them.

"Good afternoon, Jakob. My commiserations on the death of your father. He was a good man."

"Thank you, Mr Rosen. His is a great loss."

"Please allow me to introduce my nephew, Flying Officer Gustaw Beaumont. His mother is my sister."

Jakob glared at Gus in his RAF uniform.

"I said we are all Jews. And he's a Pole," insisted Theodore. "He speaks Polish just as well as you do. And your young friends, Jakob?"

"My cousin Dawid showed you in. The other three escaped from Nazi Germany. We're all Lehi," said Jakob. "It's better for all of us that you don't know their names."

"Lehi? The Stern Gang, eh? Well, what has the struggle come to?"

The young men remained silent.

"Lehi," explained Theodore to Gus, "are a breakaway sect from —"

"We are not a sect!" exclaimed one of those seated.

"— a breakaway from Irgun. As if Irgun is not extreme enough. They want to get rid of the British by whatever force is necessary. Once that's done, I'm sure they'll wage war on the Arabs."

"Look, Mr Rosen," said Jakob, now standing, "we are fighting for a Jewish homeland. You know what's happening in Europe?"

"Of course, I know," said Theodore, "and I want a Jewish homeland just as much as you. We all want a Jewish homeland! We differ on how we go about securing it."

"Shut up, old man!" shouted Dawid.

"No, you shut up!" shouted Gus. "You treat my uncle with respect, and if you don't, you'll answer to me!"

The Lehi fighters were silent for a moment.

"Let's sit down, all of us," said Jakob. "Please, Mr Rosen, have this chair. Walther, fetch us some liquor."

One of the young men walked out of the room into the back of the house to find the drink Jakob had asked for.

"You see Walther there?" asked Jakob, once he was out of earshot. "He's a Jewish refugee who fled Nazi Germany with some of his family in 1938. His father and two elder brothers didn't make it. They were rounded up and sent to the camp at Sachsenhausen. Do you know of Sachsenhausen, Mr Beaumont?"

"No. But please, if we're going to talk reasonably, call me Gustaw, or Gus."

"Well, Gus, the camp at Sachsenhausen is located thirty-five kilometres north of Berlin. It was established in 1936. They execute people there. Actually, the camp is used to perfect the most efficient and effective execution methods."

Gus blanched at the thought.

"During the earlier stages of the camp's existence, the executions were done by placing the prisoners in a small room, often with music playing. They called the room the *Genickschussbaracke*…"

"What? My God!"

"Oh, you understand German then? Yes, *Genickschussbaracke*, the concentration camp. The prisoners were told they were to have their height and weight measured in there. Instead they were shot in the back of the neck through a sliding door located behind them. This method was found to be far too time-consuming. So the Nazis trialled killing either by hanging or by shooting Jews in front of a trench which the bodies fell into. This more easily enabled group executions, but it created too much initial panic among the prisoners. It made them harder to control. So small-scale trials of gassing were designed. The Jews were told they were going into the shower-room, to keep them calm. These trials proved that gas chambers facilitated the means to murder the largest number of Jews without excessive initial panic. Simple, isn't it?"

"My God!" said Gus again, horrified by what he was hearing.

"Anyway, Walther found out a month ago that his family have now been moved to Auschwitz. There are even more executions there. He's sure they'll be dead by the end of the year."

Walther came back with a bottle of translucent spirit and some glasses. He placed them onto a low table and Jakob, the host, poured.

"Izaak, now tell our friend Gus your story."

"My name is Izaak Kalecki. I too am Polish, from Krakow. I was seventeen years old when the Nazis rolled into the city. They soon started rounding up the Jews. They came for my family. My father tried to resist, but they shot him dead. My mother and sisters were taken away. I hid, then made a run for it. I went through Slovakia, Hungary and Romania. It was difficult. All of them are allies of Germany, or client states. Eventually I made my way to Bulgaria, then Greece."

"That's some journey," said Gus.

"Yes. A difficult journey. I was forced to travel at night, sometimes stowing away on a train, often walking. By day I hid. In barns, trees, ditches, anywhere I could. I strangled a German soldier so that I could take his rifle. Then I killed two more Germans and a Hungarian border guard."

"And reached Greece?" asked Theodore.

"Yes. In Greece I had a choice. I could have gone from there to England and joined up with the Free Polish forces. But I chose to get to Turkey, then Syria and finally here. The promised land."

"And your family?" asked Gus.

"I don't know," said Izaak, "probably dead. Gassed, shot or starved. Who knows?"

"So," said Jakob, taking a sip of the fiery spirit, "you see what's going on in Europe. You know how determined we are. We Jews need a homeland, somewhere we can be safe. We know we will only achieve a homeland by fighting for one. We will need to make things difficult for the British, engaging in battle with them, if necessary. The Arabs will fight..."

"You can hardly blame them for that," interjected Theodore. "They see it as their land."

"We don't blame them, but we know we'll have to fight them. We'll be attacked by the Arabs around us, Syrians, Jordanians and Egyptians, too. We know we will need to be ready to fight them."

"So," said Theodore, "we Jews will have our homeland. But we won't be safe in it if we steal it from the Arabs!"

Jakob looked at him and said nothing.

"But the British run Egypt and Jordan, and the French control Lebanon and Syria," pointed out Gus.

"Once this war is over, the British and French will pull out," said Dawid. "Mark my words, fighting the Nazis will cost Britain and France a fortune. They simply won't be able to hold on to their Imperial territories. You wait and see: the second half of our century will be the time of independent new countries."

"Dawid is right," said Jakob, "and we will be one of the first. And there could be a part to play for you, Officer Beaumont."

"For me?"

"Our new country will need an army, and we'll be the core of it. But we'll need an air force as well. We'll need experienced Jews to advise us and help us organise."

The following day Gus drove Theodore to Bethlehem and on to Hebron. They walked along the long and narrow market street, flanked on each side by stores selling everything under the sun: spices, leather products, sweets, vegetables, meat. On one corner there were at least four sellers of pigeon, alive and dead. Gus spotted ceramic pottery decorated with cardoon designs. He examined the intricate, thistle-like patterns in the glaze.

"The leaves and flowers of the cardoon plants," said Theodore. "You'll see them represented in the designs of lots of Arabic ceramics."

Towards the end of the market street was the Ibrahimi Mosque, an enormous, white stone building with two minarets. Theodore took a seat at a café.

"I'll wait here. We can have coffee when you have finished. Go up to the entrance. Speak English to them. Somebody will understand. If they ask your religion, say Church of England. They appreciate neither Jews nor atheists."

Gaining entrance to the Mosque wasn't difficult. Of course, it was obvious to everyone that Gus wasn't Muslim, but his RAF uniform together with his impeccable English and good manners gained him access. He was even provided with an English-speaking guide. After removing his shoes, Gus walked into the room that allowed viewing of the cenotaph of Abraham. He noticed a small niche near the door.

"What's that?" he asked Kaleem, the Arab guide.

"There you can see a footprint, Sayidi." The guide pointed to a mark in the floor.

"Whose footprint is it?"

"This is the footprint of the Prophet Muhammad. However, I must respectfully add that the Jews believe it was created by Adam."

"And the Christians? Who do they believe made the footprint?"

"I really could not say, Sayidi."

"They think it's Adam's print, don't they?"

"As God wills it," said the guide.

They moved on. Gus peered through a metal grate in the corner of the mosque. Through it was the cave in which the three patriarchs, Abraham, Isaac and Jakob were believed to be buried.

Kaleem's route home took him past the café where Gus now sat drinking coffee with his uncle. Kaleem didn't wish to speak to the Englishman again. He didn't want to answer any more awkward questions. Obviously, the Christians believed Adam had made the footprint. Whenever did Christians recognise the Prophet Mohammad? He could see the Englishman believed none of it. And there he was, drinking coffee with a Jew.

No, Kaleem didn't want to converse with the non-believer again. He kept to his own side of the street. His gaze focused fully ahead, Kaleem strode past the two men. Kaleem, a self-taught scholar and guide in the Ibrahimi Mosque, considered the English to have brought nothing but trouble for him, his family and his people. He knew that Arabs had lived in Palestine for generations. In his grandfather's day, the Arabs had been ruled by Turks of the Ottoman Empire. Prior to that, Palestine had been ruled by various Caliphates and empires such as the Romans and the Egyptians. Those Caliphs and Turks were Muslim, but as the birthplace of both Judaism and Christianity, the land had long been home to Jews and Christians as well as Arabs. That situation had rarely been a problem, except when the English and other Europeans had become involved.

Since the end of the Great War, Palestine had been ruled by the English. Kaleem had seen with his own eyes how they had brought only discord. During the war, the English had encouraged the Arabs to rise against the Ottoman occupiers. They had negotiated with Hussein bin Ali al Hashimi, the Sharif of Mecca. They gave him an undertaking to form a united Arab state in exchange for the Great Arab Revolt against the Turks.

But Kaleem knew that the English were duplicitous. The Arabs had kept their side of the bargain, helping to drive the

Turks from Palestine. Meanwhile, the English had secretly plotted with the French to carve up Palestine and the Levant between them. Simultaneously, they gave assurances to the Jews in America, promising to establish a Jewish national home in Palestine. Now the country was full of Jews, many of whom were arming themselves and preparing to fight to rid the land of Arabs like him. With these thoughts rushing around his head, Kaleem walked home, where he sat on a comfortable cushion and enjoyed a cup of coffee with his sons.

CHAPTER 16

Like a bad penny, thought Gus, Titus bloody Grindlethorpe had to turn up at the worst possible moment. Malta had been subject to attack from enemy bombers based in Sicily for more than a year. Although some Luftwaffe units had been withdrawn to support the invasion of Russia, it mattered little. The night attacks were relentless. Gus arrived on the island in late September, posted to a newly formed fighter unit. He quickly learned that the RAF fighter squadrons defending Malta had proved too much for the Italians in daylight raids and so the Regia Aeronautica, and what remained of the German bombers, had switched to night raids. That, it seemed, had given Sir Hugh Pughe Lloyd, the Air Officer Commanding in Malta, a problem. He didn't have night-fighter capacity.

Lloyd had made the decision to form a dedicated night flight, the Malta Night Fighter Unit, based at RAF Ta Kali. The flight used twelve Hurricane IIs from Lloyd's existing squadrons. Lloyd now needed experienced night-fighter pilots and Gus, who had months of experience flying Boulton Paul Defiants against the Luftwaffe, seemed made for the posting. Sir Alex Peacock, an old friend of Lloyd, had helped him out. Lloyd also tried to sort out the island's many deficiencies in ground organisation and defence. This was where Squadron Leader Grindlethorpe featured. He had been posted from Britain and put in charge of ground defence at RAF Ta Kali where three thousand British soldiers, supported by thousands more civilians, had been drafted to better protect the Maltese airfields. Gus had to admit that Grindlethorpe seemed to be doing a good job, on the surface at least. Dispersal strips were built, and repair shops were moved underground. Covert shelters were also created in the belief that the Luftwaffe would soon return. Even technical staff, clerks and flight crews helped when required.

Now Gus stood in the sticky heat of Grindlethorpe's office at RAF Ta Kali as the squadron leader prowled around the room.

"The searchlight crews need better training," said Gus. "It's no use them holding a Ju-88 in their beam —"

"And why is that, Flying Officer Beaumont?" interrupted Grindlethorpe.

"The 88s are too fast for the Hurricanes to close down, sir. Anything else, an He-111 or just about any Italian plane, that's a different matter. Your crews need better enemy aircraft recognition training, sir."

"And what do you know about bloody searchlights, Beaumont? Nothing, that's what!"

"I'm simply telling you what it's like up there."

The Night Fighter Unit's Hurricanes usually operated in pairs — leader and wingman. The preferred method was for a pair to work in conjunction with the ground-based searchlights. The searchlight would seek out a target, keeping the enemy aircraft firmly in its beam once it had done so. Then the pair of Hurricanes would pursue it, the leader attacking at the optimum point.

"I don't need to know what it's like up there, Beaumont. I need to know what it's like on the ground. Co-operation on the ground is my main responsibility. My job is to organise co-operation between the searchlight crews and the ack-ack guns. Do you see?"

"Well, that's not going brilliantly, is it, sir?"

"What the bloody hell do you mean, Beaumont?"

"Close co-operation needs to be supported by rigorous training in communications, sir. What you're doing at present is next to useless."

"And you are an insubordinate upstart. You are nothing but a bloody troublemaker. It's a stupid idea and I'm dismissing it. Just as I'm dismissing you, Flying Officer Beaumont. Off you go!"

Grindlethorpe folded his arms. There was no use arguing, thought Gus, as he saluted, about-turned and made his way out of the squadron leader's office.

"Just think yourself lucky that you're not on a charge, Beaumont!" shouted Grindlethorpe after him.

Grindlethorpe was a hindrance, but Gus also met an old friend at RAF Ta Kali. Flying Officer Stewart 'Poorly' Poore, who Gus had trained with at the outbreak of war, was there. They spent many happy hours in the officers' mess reminiscing.

One night, Gus was flying a patrol as the wingman to Poore. It was a bright night, and the pair of them were soaring through the moonlit skies over Valletta. Suddenly, Poore's voice came over the RT. "Bandit at four o'clock."

Gus looked and saw a solitary Fiat Br-20M bomber, illuminated by searchlights. The searchlight team were doing a good job of keeping the Italian aircraft in their beam.

"I'm going after him, Bouncer," said Poore. "Keep an eye out for any others. Tally-ho!"

"Roger that, Poorly."

Gus watched as Poore's Hurricane closed in on the Fiat bomber. Suddenly the air around the two aircraft exploded in a maelstrom of fire, smoke and metal parts. Both the Br-20M and Poore's attacking Hurricane were consumed in flames as ack-ack fire from the Ta Kali base ripped into them.

Gus was dumbstruck. There was nothing left of either plane. The sky was empty. He landed, jumped out of his Hurricane and dashed over to the guns, demanding to see the officer commanding them. It was a young Royal Artillery lieutenant named McCann.

"Which guns opened fire?" shouted a fuming Gus.

"Just number four section, sir," replied McCann, perplexed.

"And you gave the order to fire?"

"No, sir. I could see the Hurricane was closing in. It was far too dangerous to open fire."

"Then who the bloody hell did?"

"I've spoken to Sergeant Harris," said McCann. "He says he heard an order to open fire."

"Let's talk to him again," said Gus, and away they strode.

Harris insisted he had been given the order to open fire. "Plain as plain can be, sir," he said. The bombardiers and gunners backed him up. Many of them had also heard the order shouted out.

"Harris is a steady man, sir," said McCann. "I'm sure he's telling us the truth."

"Who could possibly have given that order? Did you see anybody around, Lieutenant? Anyone at all?"

"Only Squadron Leader Grindlethorpe," McCann replied, "doing his rounds as usual."

CHAPTER 17

It wasn't only Grindlethorpe who caught up with Gus in Malta. He hadn't been based anywhere long enough to receive mail since he'd crashed onto Corfu. Now, the post arrived.

Dear Bouncer, my dearest boy,

How are you? All well, I hope and trust.

I have two pieces of bad news, Gus. Bad news doesn't land easily, so it's better to be out with it.

First: sadly, Ma has passed away. It was sudden. A heart attack. At least it was quick and she didn't suffer.

Second: I've had a bit of a setback myself, so to speak.

I know you well enough to realise that you like the longer version of a story, so here it goes. I've not much else to do, to be honest, than tell you my saga. You'll find out why by reading on.

A month or so ago all was well and I was sitting in the canteen of No. 2 Ferry Pool at Whitchurch, a nice cup of tea and a copy of the Express beside me. The newspaper headline told a story of woe from Greece. Athens had fallen to the Germans and British forces were in retreat to Crete and I thought you must be caught up in that somehow. I wondered where you were, if you were still alive. 'Oh, buck up, Bunty. Of course he'll be all right,' I said to myself.

I looked at my wristwatch. Half an hour until take-off. I took a sip of tea and set about reading the details. A Nazi motorcycle battalion had outflanked the British rearguard. Now it looked like the army was preparing to evacuate to Egypt. Another bloody Dunkirk, I thought. Oh, bugger this bloody war.

I wiped my lips once I'd finished the tea and joined the other pilots as they walked towards the Avro Anson that would take us to our first flights of the day. The Anson taxied to the runway. The throttles opened, engines roared and soon it was racing along the runway — well, as much as an Anson can race. No sooner was it in the air above Bristol than it levelled, turned north and began a descent to Brockworth Aerodrome. Home of the Gloster Aircraft Company.

There I walked over to a refurbished Armstrong Whitworth Whitley I was to deliver to 502 Squadron, a bomber unit based at RAF Aldergrove in Northern Ireland. I climbed into the cockpit and, with the assistance of the ground crew, started up the engines and razzed the throttle a little to ensure they were warmed up. I waved the crew away and taxied to the leeward end of the strip. Opening the throttle fully, I heard the tremendous roar of those two Rolls-Royce Merlins. Unmistakable!

A Whitley usually has a crew of five, occasionally six, but of course, I was alone on that flight. I could see cloud forming so I stopped climbing at about one thousand feet. That would keep me under it. I levelled off and adjusted my speed to a hundred and seventy knots. Soon the cloud thickened and lowered into a fog and I was finding it really difficult to see. I noticed beads of sweat on my face; I must have been worried. I was certainly finding it difficult to navigate through that blasted fog.

We hadn't been trained to use the wireless navigation system and all I could do was to fly lower and lower as the cloud level dropped; but I just could not seem to get under it. It was then I noticed flames coming from the port engine. The Whitley was low when the fire started. Now it lost height alarmingly. I didn't know where I was. I saw a large town ahead of me and was determined not to let the plane land in an urban area. I struggled with the controls, desperately trying to keep the Whitley in the air for long enough to clear the houses. Next, there was an almighty crash, and everything went black.

I awoke in a hospital bed. The nurses told me I'd been unconscious for almost two weeks. I couldn't move my legs, Gus. Then I was moved to the Emergency Medical Services unit at Winwick. It was a simply awful journey, bumping and jolting along in a military ambulance.

Soon the time came for me to speak to the doctor who had been supervising my care. Dr Dickens is a good-looking man with a stern face and, it seemed, he didn't have good news for me. I gritted my teeth in awful anticipation, Gus. My head was already spinning. I knew it wouldn't be good news. He shook his head and told me, bluntly, that I have a broken back. The damage involves my spinal cord, Gus, and, frankly, the prognosis isn't good. The break seems to have cut off communication between my brain and my body below the level of my injury — in my case, quite low down the spine. My legs aren't broken, they just won't work. I may be paralysed for life. I asked Dr Dickens if I would walk again, but he said it was hard to say right now. Occasionally some patients may retain certain sensory or motor functions. Others recover partial movement. I asked him how long that might take, but he said that, to be honest, he had absolutely no idea. He told me he was sorry, but only time would tell.

Then I shouted at him, Gus, and I began to cry. 'You bloody well should know! You're a specialist, after all!' I yelled. I'm ashamed of it now, but I was so bloody frustrated.

He said he wasn't really a specialist at all. He's attached to the neurology and peripheral nerve injury unit and in his spare time is expected to look after the patients with spinal injuries. Like me. He apologised and promised to do his best. That's all he can do, I know.

He's called Percy. Percy Dickens. Nice name, isn't it?

Percy told me that we need to allow time for the fracture to mend. I'm young and otherwise healthy, so that ought not to take too long. Then we can assess what movement is retained. There's no set-up for proper rehabilitation and therapy, which is what I'll really need. I'll need to regain strength and relearn how to do all the things I used to take for granted. I'll need to learn how to adapt to these new, limited abilities and work out how to live independently. Well, as independently as possible.

As you know, Gus, I've been used to looking after my disabled mother. Now Ma's gone and it's me in the wheelchair.

To be honest, Gus, I didn't know whether to write to you at all. I know you'll want to visit, if you can, but I'm not sure I'm ready for that. So, please wait for me to write again, won't you?

As I write this, thinking of you, I sensed the faintest sensation of tingling in the toes of my left foot.

I have to go. I hope you will get this letter, Bouncer. Sometime or other.

Look after yourself,

Bunty X

CHAPTER 18

The week had been as uneventful as usual and so Gus was excited when, early in the afternoon, Tommy Sinclair, a flight lieutenant who was acting as the unit's adjutant, summoned him and Edward 'Gobby' Gibbons to his office.

"Gobby, you've flown Blenheims before, haven't you?" said Sinclair.

"Yes," replied Gibbons.

"I know you have, Bouncer. Fancy a weekend in Algiers, the two of you?"

"Rather," said Gibbons.

Gus thought there must be a catch and there was.

"I want you to fly down to Maison Blanche in one of the Blenheims from 113 Squadron. You can stay the weekend there, but you're to be back on Monday evening, before dark, certainly. And you'll have some passengers and a new kite. There are two new pilots for the unit; Gobby can bring them back in the Blenheim. Bouncer, I want you to fly a Bristol Beaufighter back for us. It's the latest radar-equipped night fighter. We want to see how it does in Mediterranean conditions."

"Spiffing, Tommy! Thanks very much," said Gibbons.

"Oh, and by the way, 113 can't spare a gunner, or ammo. So you'll need to get a shift on to outrun any Jerry fighters. But we'll send up an escort of Hurricanes once you radio in on Monday. Can't afford to lose that Beaufighter!"

The pair dashed to their quarters. Gus sorted out the smartest uniform he could find and packed it into a small suitcase along with his RAF paybook and a few bits and bobs.

Soon the two airmen had reported to 113 Squadron, where a Blenheim was ready for them.

"We'll be looked after at Maison Blanche," said Gibbons. "43 Squadron are there. I was with them last year."

"Great! You want to fly us over?"

"I don't mind. I'll pilot, you navigate, if you like?"

"Agreed," said Gus, who already had a map in his hand.

It took less than four hours to fly from RAF Ta Kali to Maison Blanche Airport. Gibbons took off and, knowing he had nothing with which to defend them, he gained height then put the Blenheim into a shallow, top-speed dive. Once well away from Malta, Gibbons slowed to a cruising speed of a hundred and seventy knots.

As they flew over Maison Blanche, Gus looked down through the bomb aimer's window underneath the aircraft. Scores of aircraft, some of them moving around, littered the base. "It's like Piccadilly bloody Circus down there," he announced over the RT. "Take it easy, Gobby." Once parked up in the visiting aircraft park, Gus and Gibbons headed for 43 Squadron's mess. The officers there were so pleased to see Gobby Gibbons that they opened bottles of champagne in his honour.

"Let's not waste the evening on base," declared a flight lieutenant.

"How about we go into town?" suggested another, to which cheers erupted.

After a quick bath, Gus changed into the best form of RAF uniform he could muster. Instead of the usual 'Mediterranean' shorts he wore a pair of carefully pressed blue-grey trousers. He also fastened a necktie around the collar of his short-sleeved white shirt and put on a smart forage cap in place of the ragged side-hat he often chose to wear around his home base. He joined Gibbons and a group of officers clambering into two cars, and off they drove to Algiers. First they made for the Kasbah, long known as a notorious refuge for stateless folk from all over Europe and North Africa. All they found was a neighbourhood of narrow, unlit streets. Not much activity for a bunch of young flyers. No sign of the scintillating night-time entertainment Gus had imagined.

"This is a bloody dead end you've brought us to," complained Gibbons to the flight lieutenant whose idea it had been.

"Don't worry. We'll go to the American Services Club, instead."

Off they went. The club, they discovered, only stocked fizzy American beer. They were rationed to two cans of this each, which they soon downed. Gibbons decided to approach a couple of friendly US Air Force officers at the bar, and ask where the nightlife was.

"Why, the best dive in town is a place called the Sphinx. It's got wine, beer, French music and women," said one of the Americans with a broad grin on his face. He began to give them directions. The street on which the Sphinx was situated was much busier than the Kasbah. There was even a small gaggle of men waiting to go inside. A tough-looking doorman stood outside the entrance to the club. The officers found that all he wanted was money. Some tipped him British pounds or French francs retained from excursions earlier in the war. Others tendered US dollars. The doorman took anything and everything, not giving a smile in return.

Inside, Gus was crowded by what seemed like hundreds of men wearing the uniforms of every force in the Western Alliance — Free French soldiers, American airman, Australian sailors. The RAF and British army were well represented.

There were civilians, both dark-skinned and light, all in Western dress.

There was music in the background but it was difficult to hear over the cacophony of voices talking, laughing and shouting. At the bar, a hoard of customers jostled and demanded service in a variety of languages. Gibbons came up to Gus with a large glass of Pernod. "This is a bit of all right, eh, Gus?"

"Lovely, Gobby. Almost perfect!"

A large woman with heavy make-up and peroxide hair approached them. Her ample body was squeezed into a dress that might have better suited a slender ballerina.

"Good evening, gentlemen. My name it is Désirée. Welcome to the finest *maison de passe* in Algiers. You have come to the right place, I can assure you. Now, what do you prefer?"

Gibbons turned to Gus. "What's a bloody *maison de passe* when it's at home?"

"I think the lady means a brothel."

"What?"

"It's a brothel, Gobby! Wake up!"

Gibbons looked around. Women in various states of undress adorned the seating at the back of the room. One wore a low-cut basque of red silk, edged with black. It had a lace-up front and thin black straps going over her slim shoulders. She smiled invitingly as Gibbons looked at her. "Jesus Christ," he said, "what would my mother say?"

Gus wasn't listening. He was staring at a woman on a tall stool at the end of the bar. An attractive woman who, apart from her dark auburn hair, was the image of Eunice Hesketh.

Gus left Gibbons to the delights of the madame, Désirée, and made his way to the end of the bar, careful not to bang into anyone and spill their drink. He'd seen far too many scuffles and fights break out that way. As he did so, he noticed the woman beginning to write on a small piece of notepaper. The hubbub of noise in the Sphinx grew louder, boosted by an accordion player who had started up on a small stage. Gus stood right beside the woman so she would hear him.

"Eunice!" he said, almost shouting. "What the bloody hell are you doing here?"

"*Je ne parle pas anglaise, monsieur,*" the woman replied.

"I apologise, *mademoiselle,*" said Gus in his passable French. "You look so much like someone I know."

"Is she pretty?" asked the woman, with a hint of a smile.

"Would you like a drink?" he offered.

"Kir Royale, please."

Gus stared at her. That had always been Eunice's drink of choice. "What is your name?"

"I'm Clarice."

"Gus Beaumont," he said, taking her hand and immediately feeling a scrunched-up piece of paper being pushed into his palm.

"Actually, I won't have that drink, thanks. I really must go, maybe another time? Goodbye, *monsieur!*"

Gus watched as she cleared a swaying path to the door and walked up the steps to street level. Then she was gone. He opened the piece of paper she'd given him. It read:

It's me. I can't talk here.

Meet me outside in half an hour.

"Tell me," Gus whispered, as he and Eunice sat on a small seat in a pretty garden, "are we speaking English now? Or is it French?"

"English is fine so long as nobody's around. If anyone comes along, we'll move."

"Not that it isn't nice to see you, Eunice, but what the hell are you doing in Algiers?"

"Actually, I'm waiting for a flight to England."

Gus waited for her to say more.

"I can't say much," she blurted.

"Then say *something*."

"I'm doing some undercover work, but I've got other news. You remember Duncan Farquhar?"

"Of course," said Gus. "Duncan's an old friend from university days. He was with the Ox and Bucks, then transferred to the Royal Engineers. I bumped into him at Calais and…"

"He told me. Duncan was taken prisoner at Calais, during the evacuation," she said.

"Better than being killed."

"He was sent to a POW camp in Germany, but he escaped. Isn't that wonderful? He made it to France, handed himself in to the Resistance and he's now in Spain."

"That's fantastic, but how do you know?"

"And your friend Professor Bloch. I think he's also alive and well, working with the French Resistance."

"Eunice, stop playing games with me. How on earth do you know all this?"

"I parachuted into France as an agent."

Gus's brows shot up. "So you decided to work for Peacock, after all?"

Eunice looked at him searchingly. "Yes. I know you don't like it, but…"

"You have to do something. Yes, I know."

"I met Duncan in France and escorted him as far as Perpignan on one of the escape routes. We met Bloch in Lyon. Well, I can't be absolutely sure it was him, but I'm convinced we did. He's part of the Resistance group there. Anyway, I handed Duncan over to a French guide in Perpignan and she took him to the border. We received a message later telling us he made it to Spain."

"How did you end up here, in Algiers?"

"A pickup near Lyon. The plane was supposed to fly back to England, but the weather had changed; the pilot had a dicey flight down and he decided to change course. The Resistance had managed to top the plane up with petrol, so he flew south to Maison Blanche."

"What type of aircraft was it?"

She looked puzzled. "A Lysander. Why?"

"Do you know who commanded the operation?"

"No."

"Did you meet an officer called Hugh Heslop?"

"This is beginning to sound like an interrogation, Gus. What's it all about?"

"Nothing. Forget I mentioned it." Gus was pleased that Peacock and Heslop had taken his advice. They were using Lysanders to collect agents, maybe to drop them too, though Eunice said she had parachuted into France. The SOE work must have started in earnest. He had a sudden desire to hurry back to Blighty and get involved with Peacock's night-flying escapades.

They walked over to the boulevard overlooking the port. The night was clear and warm and the port was busy with Allied shipping, a sign that the war must be going well. They chatted for a while, about old times in Oxford before the war, and London. Gus thought it interesting that both he and Eunice were working for Peacock now. Of course, Peacock must have known they were friends, former lovers. Peacock knew everything. He noticed that Eunice divulged nothing about the special operations and decided not to quiz her too much. But there were things he desperately wanted to know. Then suddenly, she had to leave.

"I can meet you again tomorrow, if you can get away? One o'clock at the Brasserie l'Orient, opposite the railway station?"

"Perfect," said Gus. "You can tell me what you've been up to, so long as you don't reveal anything too secret, of course. Careless talk costs lives and all that."

CHAPTER 19

The following morning Gus hitched a ride into town in a supply lorry that bumped and lurched its way towards the station. He saw the Brasserie l'Orient from the lorry. Eunice was sitting outside in a quiet corner, a pink Kir Royale on the table in front of her. He beckoned the driver to stop and jumped down.

"We're going back at about five, sir. Shall we pick you up?"

"You'll come this way?"

"Yes, sir."

"If I need a lift, I'll stand here. If I'm not here, don't worry — I'll make my own way back."

The driver gave a wave and drove slowly away. Gus walked over to Eunice, took a seat next to her and called for a cold beer.

"Ever done a parachute jump, Gus?" asked Eunice.

"No. Gone through the whole process, of course — part of my pilot training. But I've not done it for real. Not yet."

"I tumbled out of that aeroplane into a clear sky, illuminated by bright moonlight. It was simply beautiful, Gus. Shall I tell you all about it?"

"Yes, I'd like to know."

"My hair was dyed auburn. I clutched a tiny carry-case packed with papers in the name of Clarice Delacroix."

"Clarice suits you very well."

"I clambered aboard a converted Armstrong Whitworth Whitley bomber, its two engines already ticking over. After what seemed like hours, I was beckoned to the 'Joe hole' by a smiling flight sergeant. He was still smiling as he pushed me out into the night sky. A blind drop. Nobody would be there to meet me at the landing site, or get me to a safehouse." She took a sip of her Kir Royale.

"Damned dangerous, if you ask me," said Gus. "A blind drop into a deserted Normandy field. At least, you must have hoped the field would be deserted."

Eunice nodded. "It was. Though I had the nagging thought of a Nazi reception committee. There is always that risk. Then the static line jerked my parachute open, and I felt the pull at the webbing straps. My descent slowed and there I was, hanging over occupied France. I peered through the darkness, trying to spot anything that might hinder my landing and glide away from it; there is a constant danger of injury in parachute landings. I spotted trees, but didn't have time to think, let alone glide! I had around fifteen seconds from exiting the Whitley to landing, heavily, on the ground."

Gus shook his head. "Go back, Eunice," he said. "Tell me the story from the start, would you?"

"Well, as you know, before the war Wing Commander Sir Alexander Peacock had assessed my character and potential to work as an undercover agent. I hesitated at first, but now I wonder why. I saw our friends fight and perish in the war, and lost my parents to German bombs; I knew that I wanted to play my own part in the struggle against dictatorship. So eventually I contacted Peacock and accepted his offer."

"What was the training like?"

"It was tough, Gus. Some candidates at the prelim school fell at the initial hurdle. We never saw them again. The schedule included physical training, weapons handling, unarmed combat, map-reading, field craft and the basics of radio communication. Sometimes I hated it, but somehow I got through. Following that, I was sent to Scotland for more training. That began with a hard slog over the tough terrain in the hills around Inverness. The other women and I had to complete the same course as the men, crawling around on our bellies and trekking up mountains, all the time honing our map-reading and compass work. We were all tired and aching at the end of the day.

"Then there was the weapons training. I was taught how to use a .38 revolver and a Sten gun. I was told to always fire two shots, to be certain of hitting the target. Sabotage was also high on the agenda — demolition and explosives training using dummy explosives. I can bring a whole train to a stop, you know."

"I don't doubt it!"

"Later I was sent to Ringway, near Manchester, for the parachute course. We all did at least two jumps, one from a static balloon and one from a low-flying aeroplane. As the pilots needed to fly low into occupied territory in order to avoid detection by the enemy, jumps could be as low as three hundred feet. Following jump training I moved to Beaulieu in the New Forest. The agent training schools there covered such things as personal security, communication in the field, how to maintain a cover story and how to act under police surveillance."

"Bloody hell, Eunice! How ever did you stick it out?"

She looked at him thoughtfully. "Sometimes I wonder that, too." She took another careful sip of her drink. "Soon after that, the Eunice Hesketh you knew became the Clarice Delacroix here with you now. I was briefed by Sir Alexander at his home. From then on, I acted like Clarice, spoke like Clarice and looked like Clarice. I *am* Clarice."

"Not to me. In my eyes you will always be Eunice."

She smiled at him.

"Tell me what happened after the drop?"

"I landed with a heavy bump and twisted my right ankle. But I had to move quickly. I removed the harness and my jumpsuit, took the small spade strapped to my leg and hastily dug a hole in which to bury the parachute and jumpsuit. There had been no need to worry; the field was completely deserted. It was now the middle of the night and I had four hours before daylight. Four hours to get myself organised. I walked with a slight limp to a crossroads and studied the signpost. Being careful to keep the torchlight pointing downwards, I turned the map to orientate it. Then I made my way towards Lisieux.

"When it was light, I boarded a train at Lisieux and travelled to Paris. As instructed, I took the metro to Saint-Denis Porte de Paris and walked to the Rue de la Barbacane. But that gay and charming pre-war Paris I remembered from when I'd worked in the city as a fashion model was long gone. Paris is now consumed by the trappings of war and occupation. Walking from the metro station, I soon found the small, rundown *pension* that would be my home for a few days.

"That first night I sat in the Bar du Monde as instructed, pretending to read a copy of Victor Hugo's *Toilers of the Sea*. A Kir Royale sat on the table, just a single sip of it taken. I put down the book, gazed at the rain on the windowpanes and waited. My thoughts drifted back to 1940, before the German invasion.

"I'd reported to my contact, Xavier — not his real name — and he'd introduced me to his friends as his younger sister, Clarice. It was all a test to ensure I could pass as French."

"And could you?"

"Of course. Anyway, my train of thought was broken as a middle-aged woman opened the door to the Bar du Monde, shaking rain from her umbrella. She marched across the room and sat down at the table next to me. 'Shocking weather,' she muttered, then ordered a coffee from the waiter. She looked at my book. 'You enjoy Victor Hugo, *mademoiselle*?' she asked. 'Yes,' I answered, 'but mostly his later works.'

"'Myself, I prefer Schoelcher,' said the woman. I nodded. That was the codeword. The waiter brought a small black coffee for the woman, who added sugar to the cup and stirred. 'How's the Kir?' she asked. I told her it was fine. She said the Germans had taken most of the champagne and it was probably made with something from Limoux. 'You have the parts?' she added in a whisper, referring to the valves for a radio transmitter I'd brought from England and was to pass on to the Resistance. I told her that I did, but not with me. 'Then enjoy your drink for a while after I leave and meet me back here tomorrow evening, at seven. Bring them with you.' I must have glanced at the waiter because she whispered not to worry about him; he was one of us. She told me if I needed to contact her I was to ask the waiter. I asked what I should call her. 'L'Oiseau Chanteur,' she said. *The Songbird.* Then she drank the coffee in two gulps and stood. 'No time to hang around here all day,' she said. 'I still have some shopping to do.' She strode to the door and stepped out onto the rainy street. Then she was gone.

"The parts were in a small bag that I'd placed in a drawer of the bedside cabinet at the *pension.* The next day I opened the drawer and removed the bag. The valves were in a parcel of waterproof cloth. I put them into my handbag.

"The rain eased off as the day wore on, and so I decided to go for a walk in the city centre. I took the Metro to Barbès-Rochechouart and walked around Montmartre to the Basilica. The area was busy. Everywhere I looked I seemed to see German soldiers. I sat on a bench and gazed at the city sprawling to the south. Then a voice with a German accent spoke. 'May I sit here, *mademoiselle*?' I looked round. A German officer was politely requesting permission to sit by me. Bugger! What to do? I was frightened, Gus. Then I remembered my training. Behave as any young French woman would; don't attract attention. And do not, under any circumstances, do anything that might be misunderstood as flirtation."

"What did you say to him?" Gus asked.

"I said, '*Bien sûr, monsieur, je suis sur le point de partir,*' and with that I rose and moved away. I think he looked a little disappointed."

"I'll bet he was disappointed," said Gus, taking a slug of his beer.

"It had been a mistake to go into town, I thought. So I went back to the Rue de la Barbacane and the safety of my room in that grimy *pension*. I sat and waited for nightfall."

"Then you went back to meet — what was she called?"

"L'Oiseau Chanteur. Yes, at the Bar du Monde. I ordered a coffee. Soon she arrived and sat opposite me. She asked how I was. 'I'm fine, just fine,' I replied. And I was. She ordered a glass of white wine and then whispered that I should pass the parts to her under the table. I did so as the waiter arrived with a bottle of wine. He poured it carefully into a goblet-shaped glass. L'Oiseau drank her wine quickly, then left. She was always in a hurry."

"Yesterday you told me you'd met Duncan Farquhar in France and helped him to escape to Spain."

"Yes, that's right."

"How did he reach France?"

"He escaped from a German POW camp. He told me all about it. He jumped from a moving train, coshed a soldier and stole his uniform, then made his way to France and turned himself in to the Resistance. That's when I met him. They wanted me to talk to him, check him out. Interrogate him, I suppose."

"He's a brave man."

"The brave make their own luck."

"I suppose they do. And while all this was going on, you were still in France, working for Peacock?"

"Yes. I'd spent a bloody miserable Christmas in France. There was practically nothing to do. I'd travelled to the coast to pick up a package dropped by a lone Spitfire pilot, and I'd delivered it to my contact, L'Oiseau Chanteur, in Paris."

"Wait a minute," interrupted Gus. "This drop from a Spitfire, where was it?"

"Northern coast. Close to a place called Cucq."

"Clearing on the edge of some woods, southeast of Cucq?"

"Why, yes. Do you know it?"

"I do. And what's more, I think I may have been the pilot." Gus began to wonder if Peacock was playing games with them.

"Well, thank you for that, Gus. It was a good drop. Then, two days before New Year, I met L'Oiseau Chanteur again in the Bar du Monde. She told me my orders were written on a piece of paper which she would leave on the table. She spoke in a whisper as usual. 'We'll probably never meet again, so thank you,' she said. Alone in my dingy room, I read her note. It was curt, precise: *Arrive in the commune of Saint-Avold (Moselle, in Lorraine) on Saturday 4th January. Go to the Café des Amis for lunch and ask for Roget Dupont.*

"So on the second of January I took a train to Metz and stayed there overnight. On the morning of the third I took a taxi to Boucheporn, found accommodation for the rest of the month and bought myself a second-hand Peugeot bicycle." Eunice frowned at Gus. "What are you smirking at?"

"Oh, just the thought of you on a bike. Takes me back to our Oxford days."

"It was a very nice bicycle, thank you. Painted black, like most of the others. On the first Saturday of the year I cycled the ten kilometres into Saint-Avold and parked the bike next to the Café les Amis. It was approaching one o'clock. Time for lunch. I went inside, ordered a Kir Royale and asked for the menu. When the waiter eventually arrived with both, I told him I was looking for *Monsieur* Roget Dupont. The waiter didn't blink. 'Of course, *mademoiselle*,' he said. '*Monsieur* Dupont will be here shortly. I'll send him over to you.' I studied the menu and waited for Dupont. It was decidedly wartime fare, even worse than in Paris."

"Do you want something to eat now?" asked Gus. With the talk of food, he realised that he was actually quite hungry.

"That's a good idea. If you have time?"

He glanced at his wristwatch. "Yes, that should be all right. Can you suggest anywhere decent?"

"There's a place just around the corner. It does some pretty good tagine and they might even have some red table wine. Let's go," she said, enthusiastically. Soon they were enjoying a superb chicken tagine served with couscous, salad and pickles.

"I say, this is good," said Gus, tucking into his meal.

"Isn't it just? What do you think it's flavoured with?"

"Well, it's bursting with garlic, cinnamon and ginger."

"And harissa chilli paste," said Eunice. "Anyway, to continue my story, Dupont took me to meet this escapee at a local farm where he was hiding out. I was to interview him. I suppose the Resistance weren't sure about him. He'd been found in a German uniform, after all."

"And how did it go? The interview?"

162

"Dupont spoke a bit of English. 'Lieutenant,' he said, 'if you don't mind, *Mademoiselle* Delacroix here would like to ask you some questions.' Duncan agreed. Dupont suggested we all have coffee, and one of the farmer's daughters hurried off to fetch cups. We sat around a large oak table that filled the kitchen. I sat beside Dupont on a bench that resembled a church pew. Duncan perched uncomfortably on a stool at the table's end. Dupont told me to begin." Eunice took a sip of her wine. "I say, this wine is rather nice, isn't it, Gus?"

"Not too bad at all," he agreed.

"I told Duncan that I understood from Monsieur Dupont that he had dog tags, but no papers. Was that correct? He told me my English was excellent and asked if I'd lived in Britain, perhaps even been educated there. I reminded him that *I* was interviewing *him* and asked him to explain what had happened to his papers. He told me he'd set fire to them along with his uniform, which seemed reasonable. His accent was perfect, but I wanted some backstory. He told me he'd been captured at Calais in May the previous year. I asked was he a Regular, but it turned out he was a Territorial. Before the war, he said, he'd studied at Oxford. I asked which college. He replied Corpus Christi. Then I asked the crunch question: what had he studied? Ancient and Modern, he said. He didn't say 'History', you see. He had to be genuine. I asked him to name his tutor. He told me it was Professor Burgess. 'And did you graduate,' I asked, 'or did the war interrupt your studies?' He said he graduated in June 1939. I was convinced. I told Dupont that Duncan was who he claimed to be. Dupont relaxed and shook Duncan by the hand. He was all French and apologetic: 'We can't be too careful, you understand?' And Duncan was all English and proper. 'Not a problem, old boy,' he said.

"The coffee arrived and Duncan asked what we would do now. Dupont told me to stay at the farm until an hour before dusk, then cycle back to my lodgings. He said I should meet him at the Café les Amis the next day. By then he'd have some clothes for Duncan, and I could cycle back to the farm with them. I agreed. Dupont drank the remnants of his coffee and left."

"Bloody hell, look at the time," said Gus, glancing at his watch. "My lift will be here soon. Sorry, Eunice, but I have to go."

"Shall we meet tomorrow? I can tell you the rest of my story."

"I'm flying back to base in the afternoon."

"Breakfast, then? The Brasserie l'Orient does reasonable croissants."

CHAPTER 20

Gus and Eunice met the following morning at the brasserie and ordered coffee and croissants. Eunice then picked up where she had left off.

"I went back to the farm, handed Duncan the suitcase of clothes Dupont had given me and told him to make sure everything fitted, otherwise we could change them. Dupont said he was to grow a beard then colour it and his hair grey."

"Why grey?" asked Gus.

"The Germans would be on the lookout for men of military age. They're usually Frenchmen dodging the draft for war work in Germany. Or downed airmen, or escapees like Duncan. Anyway, when I asked him if he knew you, he was so surprised that I thought he was going to choke. He spilled coffee all over his pullover."

"Must have been a shock. Bloody coincidence, after all."

"Indeed. I handed him a handkerchief and he soon recovered. He told me that he did know you and explained that the last time he saw you was the day he was captured. He thought you'd been shot down by a Messerschmitt. I told him that you'd survived, made it back to England and joined a fighter squadron."

Eunice paused to take a sip of coffee.

"Duncan wanted to know how I knew you, but I told him that the less he knew about me, the safer we would both be. He asked me my name and I told him to call me Clarice. He said to call him Duncan. I think I may have smiled. It was the first time I'd relaxed in months."

"I suppose he needed false papers," said Gus. "The people of France are not free to move about without identification cards and travel permits."

"Quite. Nazi patrols stop and search citizens without warning or reason. I told Duncan that once his beard had grown and we'd bleached it, someone from the Resistance would come to take photographs and forge papers for him. Then we were going to move him to Paris by train. He was worried about not being able to speak French."

Gus nodded. "Yes — bit of a problem, that."

"I told Duncan that I would be travelling with him and would deal with any awkward issues. The ordinary German guards don't speak French, you see — we just needed to hand over our papers if asked and try not to look concerned. The guards would only want to see that we had papers on us, and that we looked like the photographs. From Paris we were to go south. The Resistance wasn't sure yet which route was safer. It would either be Limoges to Toulouse and then on to the Spanish border, or Dijon to Lyon and then Spain. Either way, I'd stay with Duncan until we reached the border. The French have a strong network of volunteers. We'd be hidden in private homes along the way. When I left him, he'd have to cross the Pyrenees on foot with a local guide. Once in Spain he'd be assisted by British diplomats to travel to Gibraltar, and they'd get him back to Blighty."

"More coffee, Clarice?" Gus asked.

"Yes, please."

"You make it sound like a bit of a lark," he said, topping up her cup.

She scowled at him. "It wasn't a bloody lark. It was bloody nerve-racking. And once we were into Vichy France it got even more difficult. French Gendarmes checked our paperwork, not Germans. I told Duncan to leave any conversation to me."

"It's all frightfully well organised then?"

"It has to be. There is an alternative route. Paris, then to the coast of Brittany and to England by small boat. But Dupont said it was too risky. I've no idea why. Duncan was concerned about leaving me when we reached the Spanish border. He wanted to know what I'd do. Awfully sweet of him, don't you think?"

"What did you tell him?"

"I told him that I'd do exactly what I was told to do. In the end, we took the eastern Dijon to Lyon route. Duncan, with his hair dyed and wearing a pair of steel-rimmed spectacles, was dressed in the city suit provided by Dupont. He travelled as an office manager, Étienne Pinault. He'd been supplied with papers, but with any luck they wouldn't be needed. I was his secretary. If we were quizzed, I'd explain that my boss was rather deaf and had a bad back. He'd been prescribed strong painkillers that were making him sleepy."

"How did the journey go?"

"On the leg from Paris a team of German officials joined the train to check documents. A burly guard snapped at Duncan in German. He passed his papers over. I was sitting on the bench seat facing him, looking unconcerned. The Germans weren't interested. After a few days of travelling by train in the daytime and hiding in the attics and cellars of people's homes by night, we arrived in Dijon. Our time in the city was uneventful, though Duncan had developed a cough and was running a high temperature. We stayed for three days then took a train to Lyon. The train had been going for a couple of hours when it stopped for two French policemen to climb on board. Then it slowly moved off again and the police moved down the carriages, checking papers. Eventually they entered the compartment where we sat opposite an elderly woman. 'Papers!' demanded a young gendarme. The woman dug about in her handbag, trying to find her identification documents. The police officer turned to Duncan. Duncan yawned, reached into the inside pocket of his jacket and handed his ID to the gendarme, who scrutinised it. The guard asked Duncan why he was travelling to Lyon. 'Here it is!' shouted the old woman. The gendarme looked around at her and she pushed her documents into his hands. I stood up, pushing myself close to the gendarme, close enough for him to smell the perfume I was wearing. I told him my boss and I were going to Lyon on business, which was a pity really, as I liked to go there to have a good time. I smiled at him."

"Well diverted," exclaimed Gus.

"I told him my papers were on the overhead rack, in my bag, and asked if he could reach up for it. Well, of course he could and he quickly handed Duncan and the woman their papers. I smiled at him again as he handed me the bag. I took out my papers and offered them to the gendarme. He didn't even look. 'No, no,' he said, and assured me that everything was in order. He wished me a pleasant journey.

"By the time we reached Lyon, Duncan was clearly unwell. As usual we were immediately hidden away by the local Resistance, this time on the upper floor of a large townhouse in the city centre. Our host was an elderly man. He was rather short and bespectacled, and went by the name of Chevreuse. I told him we needed to rest for a few days because Duncan wasn't well. He told me that we could stay there. He spoke very good English and asked if Duncan needed to see a doctor."

"And did he?"

"I thought so, yes. Chevreuse went out and came back after a couple of hours. With him was a woman about his age. He explained that she was a physician and that she would take a look at Duncan. He had a bag of food and other bits, which he took into the small kitchen. The doctor asked me to tell her what I could about Duncan's condition. I explained what he'd been through as we climbed the stairway. We entered a small room, where Duncan lay on a bed. He was hot, sweating but shivering. The doctor examined him and told me to get Duncan to cough. I translated and asked what she thought was wrong. She said he had some kind of infection in his lungs, maybe from the POW camp or perhaps the farm. She said living on the run wouldn't have done him any good. I asked if he would recover and she said that he was young and strong, so probably yes. She said she couldn't do much about the infection itself, his body needed to fight it, but she'd try some sulfacetamide in powder form and use quinine to help reduce his temperature. She took some powders from her case; one was ground bark from a cinchona tree, which she told me to mix with water and encourage him to drink. The other was the sulfacetamide, to be mixed in the same way. Duncan had the quinine once a day and the other medicine first thing in the morning and last thing at night. The doctor said she would come back in three days, but if he worsened I was to let her know.

"So I nursed Duncan through those three days. I mixed and administered his medicines, I tried my best to keep his fevered body cool and dry. I washed him and changed his clothes when they became soiled. By the time the doctor returned, he was awake and alert. She took his temperature, listened to his chest and smiled. She said he was normal but needed to rest for another week. When he was strong enough, we could continue our journey. But we didn't have time, Gus. We had no choice but to move on."

"What happened?"

"Chevreuse was agitated. He told me the police were getting too close for comfort. He spoke in English so that Duncan could understand. He said the police were searching the area. I asked if they knew we were there. Had they been tipped off? But Chevreuse said no. He'd been told that they were searching for Jews, names on a list. But we'd have to move. He said he would take us to his office at the university. That night, if possible. He asked Duncan if he thought he was well enough to move."

"Duncan would have insisted he was, of course."

"That's right. He said he'd be fine. So we went. We moved quietly through the dark streets, avoiding the gendarmes and everybody else. Eventually we came to a large university building. Chevreuse had keys to the outer door, which he opened and then locked behind us, and took us to his office. He told us we'd need to stay there for a couple of days. He would bring us food, and there was a wash room at the end of the corridor, but he told us only to use it between eight o'clock at night and seven the following morning. 'Never use the lights, because somebody will notice,' he said. He pointed to a bucket. He said he was sorry, but it was the best he could do. There were some blankets on the couch."

"Sounds cosy," said Gus, with a wink.

"Oh, do stop it, Gus. I need to get this whole blasted story off my chest!"

"I'm sorry, Eunice. Please, carry on."

"We didn't sleep well, as you can imagine, with all the worry. I insisted Duncan had the couch whilst I made the best of an old upholstered office chair. We awoke to find ourselves surrounded by books and papers on historical subjects, many of them by Professor Marc Bloch. Duncan spotted them first. He pointed to the books and asked if I thought that was the real identity of our friend Chevreuse. I was sure I knew the name, but just could not place it."

"Professor Bloch was the one who sent me that coded letter I asked you to translate, remember? I'd bumped into him on the *Royal Daffodil* evacuating from Dunkirk."

"Yes, of course, darling, but I'll come to that later."

"What did you say to Duncan?"

"Nothing, really. I just told him I thought it best we didn't mention it."

"Careless talk cost lives."

"So you've said before, and indeed it does. The rest of our journey was uneventful, thankfully. After bidding farewell to Chevreuse, we travelled by train to Marseilles and from there to Perpignan railway station, where I handed Duncan over to another agent. I gave him a little peck on the cheek and wished him good luck."

"He'll have enjoyed that," said Gus, grinning.

"He was guided over the border by a Spaniard and eventually would have made his way to Gibraltar and on to England."

"Do you know for sure Duncan got home?"

"No, but the most difficult and risky part of the journey was over, so I expect he did."

"And what about you? What did you do then?"

"I returned to Lyon. When I saw Chevreuse again, I suddenly recalled where I'd come across the name Marc Bloch before — from you, Gus — and I eventually put two and two together. The professor's work is well known across the world, and an elderly university academic can travel around occupied and Vichy France without arousing any suspicion."

"Yes, what a fabulous cover for an agent!" agreed Gus.

It was time to go. Eunice kissed Gus on the lips and he left to find a good wine shop. Afterwards, Gus stood by the Brasserie l'Orient, waiting for the RAF supply lorry. He had half a case of champagne to take back to the mess at Ta Kali. It was the least he could do.

CHAPTER 21

Gus and Gobby Gibbons stood with the two new pilots, both fresh from training and wearing brand new flying suits. They made ready to fly back to Ta Kali, the two new officers in the Blenheim with Gibbons, one in the rear gun turret, the other in the navigator's seat, up front. Gus had packed the champagne in the rear gunner seat of the Beaufighter.

"Strange-looking beast, isn't it?" said Don Follett, one of the new pilots.

He was right. The Bristol Beaufighter was based on the Blenheim and its stablemate, the Beaufort, but with much more powerful Bristol Hercules fourteen-cylinder air-cooled radial engines.

"The story doing the rounds," said Gibbons, "is that these monster engines caused too much vibration and so they were pushed forwards on internal struts. This moved the kite's centre of gravity too far forward and so, to compensate, the cockpit was made smaller and moved backwards."

Gus clambered into the cockpit. With its tail down, the view forward was almost non-existent.

"I can't see a bloody thing," he said. "All I can see to the sides are these massive engines."

As he spoke, the engines were started up with a deep, throaty roar. Gus went first, taxiing with difficulty, opening the throttle to get the tail up. Now he could see. He sped along the runway and as the Beau reached take-off speed, he heaved back on the stick. Once in the air, Gus circled and waited for Gibbons.

The Beaufighter was faster than the Blenheim, which could reach a top speed of two hundred and thirty knots. The Beau could make two hundred and eighty. The power of those engines could also be used to carry a heavy armament and the airborne radar equipment that the night fighter flight at Ta Kali so badly needed.

Gus and Gibbons were in action almost as soon as they returned to RAF Ta Kali. Tonight, Gus was flying as Gibbons' wingman.

"Nice clear night for enemy bombers. We could be busy," said Gus as they walked out to the strip to find their Hurricanes. Gibbons was silent, staring straight ahead.

"Did you hear me, Gobby?"

"Sorry, what was that?"

"I said it's a clear night for enemy bombers. We could be in business under this moon."

Gibbons nodded and walked determinedly to his fighter. The two night-fighter pilots climbed into their aeroplanes, went through the usual checks, then taxied onto the strip. Gibbons was first off, gunning the Merlin engine and racing the Hurricane along the runway. He took off, Gus in pursuit, and circled up to fifteen thousand feet where they both levelled off and began searching the skies for the Italians.

East of Valletta, over the leeward side of the island, the searchlights picked up a Fiat Br-20M. First one searchlight caught it, then a second, and now both held the Italian plane firmly in their beams. The Italian was right in front of and below Gibbons' Hurricane.

"Enemy ahead. Angels eleven. Tally-ho!" called Gibbons over the RT and he began to close down the Italian bomber.

"Roger," said Gus, who was on his wing.

Gibbons opened fire and Gus saw tracers streaming wide of the Italian bomber. Gibbons had fired from way too far out and his bullets were doing no damage whatsoever to the enemy plane. *What is wrong with him tonight?* thought Gus.

Gibbons peeled off to starboard. "Missed the sod. Sorry, Bouncer. He's all yours." Now Gus had his chance and he closed in. He moved closer, closer and closer still, with sweat on his brow and his mouth dry as sawdust. Gus opened fire and felt the vibration as the wing-mounted Brownings responded. Almost instantaneously, the bullets brought down the Br-20 in a blazing inferno.

The two Hurricanes came back together and searched the skies over Valletta for more enemy targets. Nothing.

"We're low on fuel," said Gibbons. "Return to base."

"Roger, you land first. I'll circle to cover you."

"Roger."

As they returned to Ta Kali, Gus watched as Gibbons turned and lined up the runway, all the time losing height. Then he saw it. "Abort!" he shouted. "Abort, Gobby. You've not got the undercarriage down, you stupid bloody idiot! Do you hear me? Abort!"

My God, thought Gus. *Gobby Gibbons has completed over five hundred combat hours in Hurricanes over France, England and Greece, but he's forgotten to lower his undercarriage before touching down.*

It was too late. Gus watched helplessly as Gibbons' Hurricane bellyflopped onto the runway and screeched its way along the landing strip. He saw it veer to port and hit a group of oil drums, whereupon it burst into flames. The ensuing blaze consumed both Gibbons and his Hurricane in a furnace of white heat.

One tiny mistake and that was it. Gobby was dead.

Gus was tired of the Mediterranean, tired of Grindlethorpe and, if he admitted it, tired of dodging and chasing enemy fighters. He needed something different. Not easier. Not any less dangerous. Just different.

CHAPTER 22

The situation with Grindlethorpe was getting worse. His main responsibility may have been co-ordination of ground forces, but the squadron leader's influence seemed to extend to just about everything in Gus's life. When the menu in the officers' mess was changed to plainer and more meagre rations, Grindlethorpe was at the bottom of it. He ordered the redecoration of the offices during a particularly intense period of enemy bombing raids, taking badly needed ground crew away from their primary roles. When Gus had a day's leave cancelled at the last minute, he discovered it was on Grindlethorpe's orders.

Gus thought that much of it was down to Grindlethorpe's personal vendetta against him. He was sure the squadron leader had never forgiven him for the death of Flight Sergeant Bernard Chester back in 1940, and the loss of that Lysander in France during the Dunkirk evacuation. Had Grindlethorpe ordered the ack-ack guns that did for Stewart Poore to open fire? If so, had the shells been intended for Gus himself? Or was he just being paranoid?

When things came to a head in October, it was over an issue which by rights ought not to have bothered Grindlethorpe at all. The unit was again finding that their Hurricanes had great difficulty in intercepting the faster Junkers Ju 88s. Gus, caught up nightly in the problem, came up with a plan.

"We need to change our tactics," Gus suggested. "Instead of trying to catch the buggers over Malta, which we simply can't do, we hit them at their home base. We know the Ju-88s are flying out from Sicily, so we could try operating night intruder missions over there. Intercept the enemy aircraft over their own airfields."

"Don't be daft, Beaumont. Your Hurricanes don't have the range," said Grindlethorpe.

Flight Lieutenant Tommy Sinclair, the adjutant, raised an eyebrow.

"We could fit them with external fuel tanks to increase their endurance."

"It's nonsense," insisted Grindlethorpe. "If we can't keep up with the Ju-88s over Malta, how the bloody hell will we tail them back to Sicily?"

"We'll tail them because they'll slow to a cruising speed on their way back to base," replied Gus, undaunted.

"Utter bloody nonsense," repeated Grindlethorpe.

"I'm not so sure," said Sinclair. "It could be worth a try. Anyway, we don't actually need to tail them. We know where their bases are."

"That's good," said Gus.

"Well, I want it on record that I'm against it," snarled Grindlethorpe.

"Noted. But as I am at present in charge of the Flight, I think we should give it a try," said Sinclair.

"Me too," said Gus. "We'll have a head start over the Jerries."

Grindlethorpe's face was a picture of incomprehension and rage.

Sinclair turned to Gus. "Flying Officer Beaumont, I'll have two Hurricanes fitted with fuel tanks and ready to go by the end of the week. As this is your idea, you can have the privilege of leading them. Who do you want as your wingman?"

"Gordon Wainwright's a good man. I'll take him, if that's all right. Can I brief him myself?"

"Yes, of course," said Sinclair.

When radar picked up a bomber raid, Gus and Wainwright were scrambled.

"We must have agents on Sicily," said Wainwright. "They've given us the co-ordinates of the bases these sods have flown from."

Gus thought he must be right. Agents were everywhere, and he wondered if Peacock might be involved there, too. Once the ground observers had confirmed the raiders were Ju-88s, the pair flew off at a steady speed to Sicily.

With no night fighters in the skies above Malta, the ack-ack had a go at the Germans and downed one of them, but that didn't stop their bombs falling on Valletta harbour. As the German bombers returned to base and began their landing approach, they were hit by the two Hurricanes. Gus dived on them first, hitting them with machine-gun bullets, then Wainwright swooped down on them, finishing off the job. Once back at base, they reported one Ju-88 destroyed and two others badly damaged.

A few weeks later, Gus and Wainwright, along with some other officers, were having a lunchtime drink in a Valletta bar. An army officer strode in, looked around and then came up to them. "I'm looking for Flying Officer Beaumont," he said. Gus examined him. The captain wore the winged dragon insignia of the Royal East Kent Regiment — The Buffs.

"That would be me. What can I do for you, Captain?"

"I have a message. From your Uncle Alex."

Wing Commander Sir Alex Peacock? *Bloody hell*, thought Gus. "Let's sit over there, shall we?" He pointed to a free table by a window. Once they were out of earshot, he asked, "What's this all about?"

"My name's Hudson," said the officer, "and I've got something from your, er, uncle. But first you must answer the following question."

"Go on."

"Where did you first meet Uncle Alex?"

"Oxford. The Turf Tavern."

"That'll do me," said Hudson. He passed Gus a small package. "Sir Alex says the cigarettes are to allay any suspicions your fellow officers may have. Good luck!"

With that, Captain Hudson upped and left. Gus looked inside. The package was stuffed with boxes of cigarettes, but then he spied an envelope at the bottom.

"What's the problem, Bouncer?" asked Wainwright, coming up to him.

"No problem, Gordon," grinned Gus, pulling out some of the cigarette boxes. "Just a gift from my Uncle Alex. Want one?"

Later on, when he was alone, he read the letter from Peacock:

Dear Gustaw,

I do hope you are well.

I received a short note from my old friend Titus Grindlethorpe the other day — complaining about you, as it happens. Wants me to send you to the jungle.

Titus tells me you are doing some flights to far-off Sicily. Well, next time you go I want you to drop this parcel of supplies and money to a British agent there. The co-ordinates are below, and any time of night will suffice for the drop. The agent will check at first light.

Thank you so much,

Sir Alexander Peacock.

P.S. Do destroy the co-ordinates and this note after reading and memorising, won't you?

Gus stormed into Squadron Leader Grindlethorpe's office, slamming the door closed behind him.

"Why on earth have you been complaining about me to Sir Alexander Peacock?" demanded Gus. "If you have any complaints about my conduct, sir, then the proper course of action is to report me to the officer commanding the flight I am attached to. Sir!"

Grindlethorpe started at the ferocity of Gus's entrance. "How dare you come in here without knocking, Beaumont!" he barked. "And I'll complain to whoever I like! Anyway, how do you know I complained to Sir Alexander?"

"That's my business."

"Well, you'd do well to mind your own bloody business, Beaumont. You've no right to criticise my preparation of the ground forces here, and you shouldn't be suggesting changes to aerial operations."

"Where were you on the night Flying Officer Poore was shot down?"

"What? That's none of your bloody business, Beaumont!"

"Where were you?"

"If you must know, I was checking the batteries, as usual. Doing my job."

"It was you who ordered those guns to open fire, wasn't it? You knew bloody well the leading Hurricane was likely to be hit. You hoped it would be me, didn't you?"

"Nonsense!"

"Admit it, Grindlethorpe! You gave that order!"

"If you really think that then you should report it, Beaumont. Go on, I dare you! If you had any evidence, you would."

"If I find that you had anything to do with Stewart Poore's death, then you'll be the first to know, sir!" said Gus darkly, and he stormed out of the office.

CHAPTER 23

A second letter from Peacock had Gus dashing from Sicily to Gibraltar, where he took a ride in a Catalina flying boat back to England. He arrived in early December, in plenty of time for Christmas, and decided to stay over in Winchester with his mother.

First, however, it was necessary to meet with Sir Alexander Peacock at Baker Street.

"Congratulations, Flight Lieutenant Beaumont," said Peacock. "A much deserved promotion. And, if I might say so, it simply couldn't happen to a nicer man."

"Thank you, sir."

"Oh, do drop the formalities, Gustaw."

"Any news about my Blenheim crew? Linton and Apps? I've been worried sick about them, if I'm honest."

"Yes, as a matter of fact," said Peacock, pausing to pull some papers from a desk drawer. "Flying Officer Linton is a POW in Italy. Apparently his leg is mending quite well. Flight Sergeant Apps managed to find his squadron and is currently enjoying the war somewhere in the Western Desert."

"That's good news. Thank you."

"As well as confirming your promotion, Gustaw, I want you to know that Squadron Leader Grindlethorpe has recommended you for the Distinguished Flying Cross," said Peacock, a small smile on his face.

Gus felt his jaw drop. "Come off it, Sir Alex. Grindlethorpe hates the sight of me."

"Quite. And, of course, he didn't recommend you. I did. What he actually said about you doesn't warrant repeating.

Anyway, congratulations, Flight Lieutenant Beaumont DFC. The main news, however, is that I've got another posting for you. One you'll like, I hope. I've requested your imminent transfer into the new Special Duties squadron — 161 Squadron — based at RAF Tempsford, but you'll need to volunteer. I can't order you."

"Thank you, Sir Alex. Thank you very much indeed. I just need a little time…"

A decision would have to wait. For now, Gus just wanted to relax.

"Of course. After Christmas, then. Yes?"

Once she had welcomed him home, Gus's mother, Magda, asked after his cousin. "When is Stanislaw due to visit?"

"Christmas Eve," replied Gus. "He can't get away any sooner."

"That's a shame. Still, it will be good to see him again. I last saw him at your father's funeral. That's right, isn't it?"

"Yes. But I've seen Staś since. I told you about it. Remember?"

"No. No, I don't recall. When did you see him last?"

"This year, just before I went to Greece."

Magda's failing memory was beginning to worry Gus. Where might it end? In other circumstances he could move closer to keep an eye on her. This blasted war prevented any planning.

"We'll go to The Royal for a drink, Albert," said Gus to his mother's chauffeur. They'd driven to Winchester railway station in the family's gleaming, black Austin Windsor saloon.

"Yes, Mr Beaumont. Shall I drive you there?"

"No, thank you. The walk will do us good. Wait here for us."

Gus spotted his cousin walking out from the station buildings.

"There he is! Staś!" he shouted.

They walked into town, their highly polished black shoes crunching on the layer of fine snow that lay on the ground. Their heavy, grey woollen RAF greatcoats protected them from the cold winter wind that blew from the east.

The streets were busy with shoppers buying last-minute gifts or looking for items of food which weren't available this time last week. The bar at The Royal was also crowded. Gus ordered half-pints of best bitter and Navy-strength rum, and the pair sat by a roaring fire.

"What have you been up to, Gus?" asked Staś.

Gus regaled Staś with tales of fighting the Nazis and Italians in Greece and Malta. Throughout, he remembered to omit any reference to the clandestine work he had undertaken on Peacock's behalf.

"And I managed to visit Uncle Theodore," said Gus.

"Really? How?"

"The Blenheim squadron was moved to RAF Aqir, in Palestine. It's not far from the Rehovot Yishuv where the Rosens live."

"How are they?"

"Good. Everyone out there seems to be doing well. It's not easy, of course. The land is difficult, but they're getting it into shape. Then I was posted to Malta. Grindlethorpe was there."

Gus related to his cousin the growing difficulties he was having with his former squadron leader. "What about you?" asked Gus.

Staś explained how the Polish squadron had been re-equipped with Spitfires, moved to RAF Northolt alongside 303 Squadron and now formed part of a Polish Fighter Wing.

"What have you been doing now the Luftwaffe has stopped bombing England?" Gus asked.

"Rhubarb."

"What?"

"Offensive fighter operations over occupied Europe. Codenamed 'Rhubarb'. Low-level strafing attacks against opportunist targets on the ground. Fighter offensive sweeps, usually escorting a small number of light bombers. Attacks on German airfields."

"It sounds a long way from the defensive operations in the Battle of Britain," said Gus.

"Yes. Then there's the 'Circus' operations. We flew over France escorting formations of twenty to thirty bombers. Sometimes as many as sixteen squadrons of fighters were up there, Gus. The idea is to provoke the Luftwaffe fighters into combat."

"Does it work?"

"To an extent. But the bombers suffered from German flak. We moved to RAF Speke in July. I visited Milly Turner."

Milly had worked as a plotter in an operation room at the RAF base in Uxbridge. She and Gus's friend Tunio Nowacki had planned to marry, but Tunio had been killed whilst parachuting from his plane over the Channel.

"How is she?"

"She's had a baby boy. She's getting along all right, but it's not easy, you know? Bringing up a child alone."

"Can't be. But she's young. She might..."

"Milly is still in love with Tunio," said Staś, prompting an awkward silence before the conversation returned to the war and planes.

"We returned to Northolt in October," said Staś, "re-equipped with the Mk Vb Spitfire."

"What are they like?" asked Gus.

"Nice. But there's a rumour about a new German fighter. A Focke Wulf that's better than the Bf-109."

They finished their drinks, put on their coats and went outside. The snow was falling a little more heavily as they strolled through Winchester's streets back to the car. Albert drove them back to the Beaumonts' home, going slowly as there was now a thicker dusting of snow covering the Hampshire lanes.

They got out of the car and walked towards the house. Staś smiled. "This is good," he said, "the sound of our shoes crunching through the snow. Reminds me of home."

"Just like Poland?" asked Gus.

"Yes, but nothing like as cold!"

"The food Mother has prepared will certainly remind you of home."

"What are we having?"

"For tonight, we've managed to find a large carp. We're having it baked in aspic, with borscht and mushroom dumplings. Christmas dinner tomorrow will be pork — we can't get a goose for love nor money — with potatoes, cabbage, split peas, and mushroom and cabbage pierogi. And we've got plenty of beer, wine and vodka."

"Then we won't starve!"

"We certainly won't starve," agreed Gus, grinning.

HISTORICAL NOTES

CHARACTERS AND PERSONALITIES

Wing Commander Sir Alexander Peacock is entirely fictitious, though I expect military types like him were scattered all over wartime London. Peacock recruits Gus Beaumont for service in the Special Operations Executive (SOE). The SOE was formed in 1940 from the amalgamation of three existing secret organisations (MI6, the Electra House Department, and MI(R), the guerrilla warfare research department of the War Office). The purpose of the SOE was to conduct reconnaissance, espionage and sabotage against the Axis powers in occupied Europe, and to aid local resistance movements.

In 1936, Beryl Markham (1902–1986) was the first person to fly solo, non-stop across the Atlantic from England to North America. She did so in a Percival Vega Gull monoplane. As far as I am aware, she did not have a goddaughter named Bunty Kermode.

Group Captain Billy Drake, DSO, DFC and Bar (1917–2011) was a British fighter pilot and air ace. He was credited officially with eighteen enemy aircraft destroyed, two shared, two unconfirmed, four probables, two shared probables, and five damaged. Drake was serving as pilot officer with 421 Flight in November 1941. Details of 421's tactics came from Group Captain 'Bobby' Oxspring's *Spitfire Command* (1984).

Marc Bloch (1886–1944) was a French historian and member of the French Resistance. One of the names he went by was

Chevreuse. Bloch joined the Resistance movement sometime between late 1942 and March 1943, after his appearance in this story. He was executed by the Gestapo in 1944.

Captain Pepe Sartori died during Operation Crusader (18 November–30 December 1941) when the British Eighth Army aimed to relieve the besieged garrison of Tobruk.

Marmaduke Thomas St John 'Pat' Pattle DFC and Bar (1914–1941) was a South African-born English RAF fighter pilot. He is credited with the destruction of around twenty enemy aircraft shot down, many of them whilst Pattle was piloting a Gloster Gladiator.

PLACES

Italy invaded Albania in April 1939 and pushed into Greece in October 1940. The Greeks, aided by Britain, had repelled the Italians by early 1941. However, this setback brought Germany into the Balkans conflict and Greece was again invaded in April 1941, leading to the occupation of Corfu and the other Ionian islands by Italian troops.

Yishuv is the Hebrew word for settlement and usually refers to Jewish settlements in Palestine before the establishment of the State of Israel in 1948.

Irgun broke away from Haganah (the main paramilitary organisation formed to defend Jewish settlements in British Mandated Palestine) during the Arab revolt against the British. It was the political predecessor to Israel's Likud Party.

Lehi, also known as the Stern Gang (from its leader Avraham Stern) was an offshoot of Irgun. It was a Zionist paramilitary and terrorist organisation with the stated objectives of evicting the British authorities from Palestine by use of violence, allowing unrestricted immigration of Jews and the formation of a Jewish state. In 1948 Lehi was involved in the massacre of Arab civilians at Deir Yassin.

In June 2022, whilst doing some background research, I visited both the Commonwealth War Graves Commission cemetery in Ramleh and Neve Shalom, where the Trappist Monastery mentioned in Chapter 15 is located.

RAF Ta Kali (sometimes Ta' Qali) on Malta was formed in 1940 and it was there the RAF regiment was formed in February 1942 when Prime Minister Churchill decreed that the RAF should take responsibility for the defence of its airfields.

Gus's weekend leave in Algiers and coincidental meeting with Eunice in the Sphinx Club is based closely on Bobby Oxspring's account (*Spitfire Command*, pp. 149–152) but I have taken a liberty with the dates. Algiers did not fall into Allied hands until November 1942 and Oxspring visited sometime in 1943.

AIRCRAFT, TANKS AND TACTICS

Descriptions of the Italian Fiat 3000 light tank and Carro Veloce CV-35 tankette seem like portrayals of obsolete, veteran armoured fighting vehicles. Yet these models were typical of the light armour of the 1930s. The Fiat was modelled on a French Renault design. Britain went to war in 1939 with the Vickers light tank and Bren Carriers. The German Panzer Mk I was comparable to the Fiat 3000 and the Mk II only slightly superior.

Fighter-bombers were known to the Luftwaffe as Jabos. They had been tried by specialist Luftwaffe units such as *Erprobungsgruppe* 210 during the Battle of Britain, but these had generally been small and low-altitude sorties. The Jabos were not much of a tactical threat — apart from the specialists — as they were notoriously inaccurate when dropping their bombs. Nevertheless, against area targets such as London they could still cause significant damage and civilian deaths.

I have the Beaufighter arrive in Malta rather sooner than the type actually did. Number 1435 (Night Fighter) Flight was strengthened by the addition of four radar-equipped Bristol Beaufighters in March 1942.

Some bombers were converted for SOE and other covert operations. A hole was cut in the fuselage for the agents to exit through. To the flight crews, all SOE agents, men and women alike, were known as 'Joes', hence the 'Joe hole' in Chapter 19.

The women flyers of the Air Transport Auxiliary are some of the unsung heroes of the war. The ATA was a civilian organisation set up to ferry new, repaired, and damaged military aircraft between factories, assembly plants, maintenance depots and active service squadrons and airfields. The pilots also transported service personnel on urgent duty and carried out some air ambulance work.

The Greek Resistance movement was one of the strongest resistance movements in Nazi-occupied Europe. It included armed partisans, known as 'andarte', and unarmed groups from across the political spectrum. The largest group was the Communist-dominated National Liberation Front, which was very active in Corfu and the other Ionian Islands.

Student protests against the occupying Italian army in Corfu took place in November 1941. I moved them to earlier in the year for the sake of Bouncer's career. High school students from all over Corfu took part in these protests, which were among the first acts of overt popular resistance in occupied Greece. Subsequently, a considerable number of Corfiots escaped to mainland Greece and enlisted as partisans of ELAS and EDES.

In the March–April 1941 Battle of Greece, British Commonwealth forces lost 903 killed, 1,250 wounded, and 13,958 captured, while the Greeks suffered 13,325 killed, 62,663 wounded, and 1,290 missing. The campaign in the Balkans came to an end the following month after German troops captured Crete. The Axis campaign in the Balkans delayed the launch of Operation Barbarossa by several weeks. As a result, German troops were forced to race against the approaching winter weather in their battle with the Soviet Union.

Gus Beaumont's flight and crash-landing of the Bristol Blenheim on Corfu which features in Chapter 7 is based on the loss of Blenheim L8511 on Corfu in November 1940. Squadron Leader J. R. Gordon-Finlayson and his crew crashed then returned in triumph to their squadron.

The kidnap of Colonel Zola is based on the kidnap of General Heinrich Kreipe on Crete in 1944. This operation is described by Patrick Leigh Fermor in *Abducting a General: The Kreipe Operation and SOE in Greece* (2014).

Aircraftman Wonnacott's favourite quote, 'an army marches on its stomach', has been attributed both to Napoleon Bonaparte and Frederick the Great.

L. T. C. (Tom) Rolt bought the converted narrowboat *Cressy* and had her fitted out as a liveaboard. In 1939 he and his wife set out from Banbury to cruise the Oxford Canal towards Birmingham. The war delayed their progress, but Rolt wrote about their adventure in his book *Narrow Boat*, published in December 1944. In 1946, Rolt, along with Robert Aickman and Charles Hadfield, formed the Inland Waterways Association.

A NOTE TO THE READER

Dear Reader.

Thank you for taking the time to read *Bouncer's Blenheim*. I hope you enjoyed reading it as much as I enjoyed writing it.

Reviews are invaluable to authors, so if you liked the book, I'd be grateful if you could leave a review on **Amazon** or **Goodreads**.

Readers can connect with me online **on Facebook** and **X (formerly Twitter)**.

I hope we meet again in Gus Beaumont's next adventure!

Tony Rea

Sapere Books is an exciting new publisher of brilliant fiction and popular history.

To find out more about our latest releases and our monthly bargain books visit our website: **saperebooks.com**

Printed in Great Britain
by Amazon